MORNA'S LEGACY SERIES

A CONALL CHRISTMAS

A NOVELLA

BETHANY CLAIRE

For Mom

Chapter 1

There's nothing quite like the soft thump against your palm as you press it against the swollen belly of pregnancy, allowing the small infant tucked safely away in its mother's womb to kick at the inside of your hand. The surreal experience filled me with joy as I pressed my hands flush against my daughter's stomach, smiling widely as tears brimmed against my eyes. I'd felt the child's movement more than once, but it didn't matter. I seemed to have the same reaction every time. My baby's baby had completely captured my heart, even if it would still be weeks before I would know she could be safely delivered without the conveniences of technology and medicine from our own time.

"All right, Mom. I'm going to step away from you now. You simply cannot keep your hands glued to my stomach every moment of every day."

I smiled as Bri stepped away, grabbing the end of the blanket as she tossed the other end in my direction, signaling at me to help fold it. "Oh, but I wish that I could. I think the babe moves even more than you did, dear, and you were quite active."

"Really? Well, I sincerely apologize. I'm beginning to feel miserable."

As if to emphasize her point, she collapsed onto her freshly made bed and threw her hands up over her head as far as her dress would allow. I kicked off my own shoes, hiking up my dress as I sat crisscrossed on the end, pulling her feet into my lap and removing her shoes so I could massage her swollen and, what were most-assuredly sore, feet.

She sighed as I rubbed her, wiggling her toes as I squeezed them, and I suddenly saw her for the little girl she'd once been. She was more than ready and capable of taking care of a child, but I found it hard to believe that she'd grown so quickly, not to mention that I was old enough to be a grandmother.

I continued to knead the arches of her feet and heels until she drifted. Once she snored lightly, I carefully lifted her legs so that I could scoot out from under them and crawled off the bed as gently as I could. I walked to the fireplace, poking the wood until the flame took a firm root over the logs once more. I curled into a small wooden chair that sat before it as I gazed into the flames before glancing about the room.

Every inch of the castle oozed magic. It could be sensed in the air. As I sat with the fire warming my shoeless toes, I could almost feel Morna's eyes watching over us across the centuries.

No surprise really, I imagined it only made sense that magic be palpable throughout the castle. It had, after all, brought

2

Bri and me both to live in this place and century when we'd been born hundreds of years in the future.

Before I traveled into the past, I'd been an archaeologist who specialized in Celtic finds and history. The Conall Clan was my specialty, the last twenty plus years of my life spent trying to find and solve the mystery behind who'd murdered them in December of 1645.

My continuing efforts to solve this mystery brought me and my daughter to the ruins of Conall Castle only one year ago, in the year 2013. I'd pestered her until she'd agreed to accompany me, not knowing that a spell cast by a beloved Conall ancestor, Morna, would rip her from our time and bring her into the past to live with the Conalls right before the devastating massacre.

Thankfully, Bri was meant to be here. Not only did she help them change the course of history by stopping the massacre, but she also fell in love with the man of her dreams, Conall Castle's new laird, Eoin. I'd been unwilling to be separated from my daughter, no matter how happy for her I was, and so when Bri decided to stay in this time, I used Morna's spell to travel back myself.

The thrill of an archaeologist's life is to be living with the very people she's devoted so much of her life to learn about. I now lived in a dream that was only slowly becoming reality. And, on top of it all, I would soon become a grandma.

I was as happy as I'd ever been with only one lingering thought keeping me from overwhelming happiness. I'd always been social, I liked to date, I liked to flirt. While it had become more difficult to find a date with someone my age even in my present day time, I was certain that in the seventeenth century, men considered me hopelessly over-the-hill with one foot deep into the grave.

I would most likely spend the rest of my days alone. Something I'd realized shortly after arriving in this time, but a fact of life that took me a bit longer to accept than I had hoped.

No matter. I had much to be thankful for. Christmas time, my favorite time of the year, had arrived. I was anxious to discuss preparations for the holiday with Bri. So when I saw her stir, I stood from my place by the fire and went to stand by her side.

* * *

"What?" I knew the pitch of my voice went too high, almost squeaky, but if that old bat thought she could stifle our Christmas she had another think coming.

"Mom, is it really that big of a deal? We didn't even notice it last year."

The hormones were messing with her head. Bri loved Christmas as much I did. I couldn't imagine how she seemed to be so fine with skipping Christmas. "Yes, it's that big of a deal! Of course you didn't notice it last year. You were all too busy trying to stop the attack on the castle. What's Mary's problem with Christmas?"

I didn't miss Bri's eyes roll before she answered my question. "She likes Christmas very much. She loves cooking, you know that. It's only that after Eoin's mother passed away, Christmas became less of an event as the years went on. Not to mention, it's been outlawed in Scotland for the last four decades."

My eyes mimicked my daughter's roll. "Darling, you know as well as I do that Christmas continued to be celebrated, just a little more quietly. Besides, who is there to enforce it when your husband is laird?"

"Well...no one really. Look, I love Christmas, but I've no desire to put Mary into more of a tizzy than she stays in constantly. If you can get her to agree to it, then I will be the first to jump on the Christmas bandwagon with you."

"Oh, I'll get her to agree. As much as she likes to fight it, I'm Mary's closest friend, and she's all bark anyhow. Go and get Eoin. While I know she will eventually get on board, we may need him to intervene in the argument she's sure to put up."

Bri nodded and laughed as I turned and left her bedchamber. It was no laughing matter. Whether the child was present or not, my first grandbaby would have a Christmas to rival any other. I would make certain of it.

Chapter 2

Three Days Ride North of Conall Castle

Snow built outside his window, and his creaky joints told him a bad storm brewed. Still, he left his home at this time every year. He'd not missed his trip to her gravesite once in the twenty-plus years since his beloved had passed away. He did not intend to let the snow deter his plans.

Hew walked around his small home, tidying up before his journey south. He lived alone, far away from the nearest village. He'd not seen another soul in months and that was just as he would have it. He knew his shyness held him back. It had been a wonder that he ever married at all.

* * *

He'd not expected it, the day his sister's best friend, Mae, had approached him while he chopped wood for the fire at the back of his home, grabbing his face and kissing him squarely on the mouth. He'd been a young lad then and that kiss had changed his life. Hew grew up with Mae constantly in their family's home. Mae and his sister were inseparable. While he silently admired her for years, he was far too shy to ever express the way his heart beat for her.

That night so many years ago, he'd been able to feel her watching him but did not turn to greet Mae, his heart pounding uncomfortably just at the nearness of her. He continued to swing his ax down into the blocks, swiftly chopping the wood into two pieces. Her hand on the lower part of his back caused him to jump, nicking the edge of the block of the wood before he threw his ax to the ground and whirled to face her.

"Mae, ye startled me, lass. Ye should be inside. 'Tis far too cold for ye to be out of doors." He could remember every word spoken between them, a scene held captive forever in his mind.

She'd touched his arm then, smiling as she shook her head, dismissing his worry. "Hew, if 'tis no too cold for ye to be out here, then I doona think I shall freeze to death either. Did ye know that I shall turn ten and eight tomorrow?"

He'd stepped away from her, too many nerves for him to stand there with her hand lying on his arm. "Nay, lass. I dinna know. I shall make ye something. Carve ye a piece of jewelry perhaps?" He didn't know what to say to her, never did.

"I would like that verra much, but that isna why I mentioned it to ye."

He'd gathered the freshly chopped logs of wood into his hands, desperate to keep busy in her presence. "Nay? Why did ye then?"

He stilled when she moved to stand in front of him, blocking his path. "Will ye set all that down for only a moment, Hew? I'm trying to talk to ye if ye canna tell."

He reddened and obeyed. "Aye, lass. Why doona we sit for a moment?"

They'd moved to the pile of wood, stacked just high enough to serve as the perfect seat. He trembled as she unexpectedly grabbed his hands, but he swallowed his nerves and forced himself not to flinch away from her touch. "What is it, lass?"

"As I just told ye, I shall be ten and eight tomorrow, and I doona wish to become an old maid."

Hew couldn't still the twitch of his hand as he realized where she headed with her words. "Nay, lass, I doona believe that ye will. There are many lads who would eagerly wed ye."

"Aye, I doona believe that I shall become an old maid, either. Still, most me age are already married. While yer sister is several years older than me, she was married at ten and seven. And ye are right, many lads would be willing to wed me, but I am no so eager to marry them."

"Why is that, lass? Is there no one that catches yer fancy?" It was too much for Hew to wish that Mae would answer as he wished, but to his everlasting shock, she had.

"Aye, there is one, and I willna allow him to behave as if he doesna care for me as much as I care for him a moment longer."

His heart began to beat so quickly he feared she could feel its quick pulse in his fingertips. Though a cold night, sweat beaded freely on his brow. "Is that so, lass? And who is this lad that ye speak of?"

"If ye doona know, ye are as daft as yer sister seems to think ye are."

She paused and reached in quickly to kiss him. He acted so stunned, she pulled away before he could react and kiss her properly. "Nay, lass. Ye canna mean it. 'Tis some other lad that ye mean and ye are simply using me for practice, aye?"

She laughed before kissing him once more. This time he pulled her close as she melted against him. Breathlessly, she pulled away from him so that she could whisper into his ear. "Nay, Hew, there is none other but ye. There never has been. Ye are going to marry me."

He smiled against her cheek, her confidence somehow diminishing his shyness. "If ye insist, lass."

"Aye, I do."

"And what shall ye do with me once we are married?" His hands found their way to her hair, and he cradled her against his chest, pulling her into a tight embrace.

"We shall move north, find a piece of land for only the two of us, and together we shall build a home where we will spend all of our days together."

* * *

They married within a fortnight and had done just as Mae wished, moving north and building a home for the two of

9

them, isolated from the rest of humanity. Five years flew by in a haze of love where they spent every moment at each other's side.

Eventually, they planned a trip to visit their families in Conall territory, but they left in winter and on their journey, Mae fell ill. She fought hard, but the sickness was too much. She died only two days after they arrived. He'd chosen to bury her close to there, in the land in which she'd grown up. With a broken heart, he returned to their home alone.

Hew saddled his horse, pushing away the memories of his past as he headed out into the storm. It had been many years since Mae passed and, while he would feel her absence always, his heart had now healed as much as it ever could from such a wrenching loss.

He continued to make the trip to her grave on the anniversary of her death to pay his respects, to speak to her, to remind himself that once in his life he had not been so completely alone.

Chapter 3

Conall Castle

I tried to make as much noise as I could as I made my way downstairs into the castle's kitchen where I was certain Mary would be busily working away on the evening meal. She knew it was me coming instantly.

"Adelle, ye doona always have to make such noise when ye move about. Come in here and help me plate the food."

I knew I didn't move more loudly than anyone else in the castle, but Mary was constantly looking for something to nag me about so I obliged her by being purposely obnoxious in her presence.

In many ways, Mary was the castle's most important resident. She'd worked in the castle for nearly forty years and everyone, especially Eoin and his brother Arran, accepted the cook and head maid as the castle's true boss. She ran the castle like the captain of a ship. Nothing happened within the walls without her notice or approval.

I stuck my head into the kitchen, smiling as I reached up into the shelf just out of her reach to grab the plates. I thought it best to test her mood before immediately jumping into what I wanted to discuss with her. "How are you today, Mary?"

Mary motioned at me to lay out the plates before she responded. "Ach, I'm fine. 'Tis a bonny day, I enjoy the snowfall, but I feel a bit of guilt for loving it so. 'Tis sure to mean more work for Kip in the stables to keep the horses warm."

"Oh, don't feel guilty about enjoying anything, Mary. You know that Eoin and Arran will both do whatever they need to so that Kip's load in the stables is not more than he can handle. I have a wonderful idea that I think we should all do together before the snow outside gathers too much."

"What might that be?"

"I think we should all go out and find a tree to cut down for Christmas!" I looked down at the plates, busying my hands as I awaited her reaction. Perhaps if I played it off as if I didn't know her thoughts on the matter, she would be more willing to discuss it.

I glanced up as Mary turned away to grab the bread so that she could break it into pieces. "Nay, I'm afraid 'tis not possible. Lovely thought though."

Mary had never in the year that I'd known her referred to anything I'd ever said as 'lovely.' I was unsure of how to respond. "Umm...why 'tis not possible?"

She didn't appreciate my attempt at an accent. "Well, Christmas is no longer openly celebrated in Scotland and, after Elspeth passed away, Alasdair dinna find the joy in the season he once did. The two lads dinna grow up with it being a grand celebration."

"Do you not enjoy Christmas yourself, Mary?" Eoin and Arran's history with Christmas seemed irrelevant. Alasdair had

12

been dead for over a year, and I couldn't see either of the men having a problem with the festivities. Their mother had died when they were very young. While Christmas might have brought up painful memories for their father, it would not have the same effect on either of them.

Mary shook her head and returned to help me with the plating of our meal. "Nay, lass. I enjoyed Christmas verra much when I was a young girl. Me brother always made me the most beautiful presents. He was quite the craftsman."

"Mary," her words surprised me. "I didn't know you had a brother. Is he…is he still living?"

"Aye lass, verra much so, but I doona see him often. He lives far away from here and is a bit shy. Always had a difficult time interacting with others. Only certain people had the ability to draw him out."

She looked down as if saddened by a past memory. I interrupted her thoughts to try and lift the mood. "Are you certain he's related to you? How could one sibling end up so shy while the other does nothing but talk?"

Mary rewarded me with a quick whack on the arm as she chuckled and resumed her work in the kitchen. "Aye, I'm certain. I suppose he was shy because I never gave him much of a chance to speak. As he grew, he simply grew accustomed to his own silence."

I couldn't help but wonder about Mary's brother, about her family, and what she would have been like as a child. I felt close to my dear friend now, but I honestly knew very little about her. She was always too busy caring for everyone else that

I was afraid we all often forgot about the woman within her. I shook my head, remembering my reason for speaking with her. "You have very cleverly changed the subject, Mary. If you enjoy Christmas, then why are you against us celebrating it? I'm sure you have some wonderful traditions you could share with us, and Bri and I could share ours as well."

Mary tried to hide the smile that pulled at the corners of her mouth, but I could sense her resolve dropping.

"I'll no say that it wouldna be a pleasant time. I just doona wish to upset the laddies if 'tis something that should bring up memories of their parents."

A deep voice in the doorway caused us to both turn our heads. I smiled as Eoin poked his head into the kitchen, Bri following shortly behind him, his strong hands resting gently on her shoulders as she lay the back of her head lovingly into his chest. "It will do no such thing, Mary. Ma made Yuletide a spectacle and, while Da did try, it wasna the same after she passed. I think 'tis far past time for us to restore the celebrations to their formal glory."

Mary let her smile pull free now, and I could see that the idea excited her as well.

"If that is what ye want, me dear lad, then I shall be as pleased as anyone. I only dinna want to upset ye or Arran."

Eoin moved across the room, each step accentuating the strength of his body, his hair even darker than Bri's and his eyes the color of obsidian glass. My grandchild was going to be beautiful.

He wrapped his arm around Mary, tucking her into the nook of his arm before bending to kiss her on the cheek. "Aye, I know. Ye are always watching out for us, and I love ye for it, Mary."

He released her and stepped away to regard the both of us. "Do ye think that the two of ye can work together to make the preparations?"

I smiled, bobbing my head up and down enthusiastically. "Of course we can." I could sense that Mary was about to intercede with some jab as to how difficult it would be for her to put up with me so I quickly spoke again, not allowing her the opportunity. "Do we have permission to do whatever we wish?" I already had a grand idea, but I didn't wish to mention it to anyone before I'd convinced Mary.

Eoin grinned and glanced cautiously at Bri. "I feel that I may come to regret this but aye, I shall no tell either of ye lassies what to do. It would be wrong of me to do so, and it would be a fruitless effort anyway."

"Absolutely right." I scooted over and draped an arm around Mary's shoulder. She glared up at me in response. "Don't you two worry. Mary and I are going to make certain this Christmas is the most magnificent Conall Castle has ever seen."

Chapter 4

"Ye have lost yer mind if ye believe for one moment that I would do such a foolish thing and follow ye into that God-forsaken time that ye came from!"

I crossed my arms and sat down on the steps leading down into the castle's basement and spell room while I listened to Mary rant. It was impossible for her first reaction to anything that came out of my mouth to be a positive one.

"What is so important that ye would feel the need to do such a thing, Adelle? I knew ye were daft but gracious, lass, 'tis a horrible idea. What if ye were unable to return home? I doona think I could stand to spend one day there."

Eventually, I interceded to stop the top of her head from exploding. "Calm down, Mary. Morna's spells are reliable. Now that we know she lives in the inn near the castle, we will go straight there to stay with her. You don't even have to go into Edinburgh with me if you don't wish. Wouldn't you like to see Morna again?"

Mary's face changed from red to white much too quickly. I was afraid I was about to have to pick her up off the ground. She extended a shaky hand in my direction, letting it hang in front of my face at eye level. "Do ye see what ye do to me? Ye have me so restless, I shall no stop shaking for days.

Nay, I doona wish to see Morna again. The lass was a dear friend, but I spent the last twenty-five years believing her dead. 'Tis where the dead should stay. Good and buried."

Breathless, she plopped down next to me. I reached out to pat her on the back but quickly retracted my hand in response to the daggers she shot toward me with her gray eyes. "She was never dead, Mary. She just moved on to a different time is all. I'm sure she would love to see you."

"Nay, I doona expect that she wishes to see me that much. If she did, could she no just come here herself to visit?"

I shook my head regretting the path I'd led our conversation. I didn't know enough about Morna or her abilities to speak of her so freely. "Never mind Morna. Don't go for her. Go for me. Surely you wouldn't want me to travel there alone?"

I was none too worried about going alone. I'd lived my entire life for the most part alone. It would be no problem for me to make the journey to my own time without her, but the temptation of watching rigid, uptight Mary in present day was a joy I very much wanted to gift to myself. It would be the best Christmas present I could ask for.

"I doona give two twiddles whether ye go alone. I hope that ye go and get stuck there. Can ye no tell by now that I'm no that fond of ye?"

I rolled my eyes at her jab. I spent most of every day at her side. If she truly didn't enjoy my company, I knew her well enough to know that she wouldn't put up with my presence. "Oh hush, Mary. If you're really so afraid to go along, that's all you had to say. I wouldn't have pressed you further. It's not good for

17

someone your age to upset yourself with the stress of fear." I winked at her. Mary was really only a few years older than me.

Mary stood abruptly and stomped her foot like a small child. "'Tis no that I'm frightened, only that ye are foolish to do so."

"I'll make you a deal, Mary. If you go, I'll help you with whatever chore you wish for the next month."

Mary hated, more than anything, beating the bed linens. I could already see her wrestling with such a temptation in the way her eyes darted back and forth, calculating whatever prevented her from saying yes. Eventually her eyes stopped moving, and I could tell she intended to speak. "Aye, fine, but I willna wear breeches that go up in between me legs. I shall stay in me dress the whole time, or I willna agree to go with ye."

I smiled. "Deal. You will look ridiculous, but it doesn't matter to me one bit as long as you will come. Let's go tell Bri and then be one our way."

* * *

Present Day

Bri had warned me that with the castle no longer being the ruins I had once known it as in present time that it had become a popular attraction with visiting tourists. Still, I had underestimated the number of people who would be in attendance once we arrived in the twenty-first century.

Mary and I had been able to make it out of the roped-off basement undetected, but the stares Mary's clothing garnered as we made our way out were enough to rival an eight-legged horse at a zoo. Luckily, Mary remained so bug-eyed at everything she saw that she remained completely oblivious to the pointing fingers and stares.

Once outside, we began the several miles walk to the inn. Mary spoke for the first time, "Excuse me language, Adelle, but holy bugger. Me head hurts something awful. I knew that it would from witnessing both Bri and yerself come through, but I dinna expect it to hurt quite so bad."

I scrunched my nose up guiltily. "Yes, I'm sorry. Morna will have something we can take, I'm certain. What do you think so far?"

"Well, I'm surprised to find that the castle looks much the same, but 'tis lighted much more and oddly."

"Yes, electricity is amazing. All homes and buildings have it."

"Is that so? As we walk along this path, it doesna look so different."

She was right, besides the gravel road leading to the castle, this part of Scotland was still very much untouched by the conveniences of modern times. "Yes, unless you decide to accompany me into Edinburgh, your shocks will be less than they could be. Morna's home will have many things to surprise you, but nothing like the city."

"Aye, well I canna say that I doona enjoy the adventure of it. Perhaps, I will join ye when ye leave for the city."

We walked in silence until we arrived at Jerry and Morna's, and I was none too surprised to find both of them waiting for us at the front door.

"Ach, Mary! I canna believe it! I nearly spit up me food when me vision showed me yesterday morning that ye two lassies were on yer way to see us."

Morna charged Mary, who blanched at the shock of laying eyes on the dear friend she'd thought lost forever. She pulled the cook into a tight embrace.

Jerry made his way over to me, wrapping his rail-thin arms around my neck. "Adelle, it is lovely to see ye again, lass."

"You as well, Jerry. So Morna saw us coming?"

Morna's voice answered me as she led Mary toward us, their arms laced with one another. "Aye, I did and I've no been so pleased by a vision in some time. I'm also thrilled to know that our dear Bri is with child, is she no?"

"Yes, and she's close to popping. Only a few more weeks, and the child will make its appearance. I simply cannot wait." I smiled, leaning in to give Morna my hug of greeting.

Morna waved us inside her home before speaking again. "I'm sure 'tis true, lass. I have something I wish for ye to take back with ye. It's an herbal potion I've mixed, 'twill help her greatly with the pains of labor."

"Oh, thank you so much. I've been worrying myself sick thinking about the ordeal she must go through. I thought I was going to die when I gave birth to Bri, and I let them drug me up with every medicine they had."

Morna laughed. As we made our way into the sitting room, Mary's eyes bulging at every odd trinket, Morna pointed at a box in the corner, and tears immediately swelled in my eyes.

"I also retrieved something else for ye, lass."

I had to keep from running toward the large box of ornaments, each a special memory of the Christmases Bri and I spent together while she was growing up. Each year our collection grew, and each new ornament was a new, precious memory. "Morna!" I hadn't a clue how to express my gratitude.

"'Tis what ye really wanted, is it no?"

I nodded in disbelief. "Yes, but it never crossed my mind that I would actually be able to get them. I just planned to go into Edinburgh and buy a brand new set. All of this was in the States, at Bri's old place. How did you...how did you do this?"

She laughed heartily. "Did I no just make it possible for the two of ye to come here from hundreds of years in the past? Compared to that, 'twas a simple task to move these to us. Look in the other box, I also included a few other things I could sense were precious to ye."

My hands trembled with excitement as I moved to open the lid of the next box. I opened it to find an old CD player that could be operated with large DD batteries, packs and packs of replacement batteries, and our entire collection of Christmas music. Bri's baby blanket, knitted by my own mother, gently padded the Christmas items. Tears fell freely at the sight of it. "Oh my God, Morna. Are you a mind reader as well?"

Jerry interjected playfully. "Aye, she is lass and 'tis damned annoying. I canna silently begrudge her anything without her finding out about it and charming me into forgiving her."

Morna laughed and leaned gently into her husband. "I am no that good at it, but ye are quite open with yer thoughts. 'Twas easy to see the things ye desired most from your trip here."

She was spot on. There was nothing more that I wished to get. Everything I thought I would be unable to find was here. As far as I was concerned, we could make our way back to the castle immediately. But as I glanced over to see Mary gleefully playing with the running water in the kitchen, I thought better of suggesting we leave right away. "I cannot thank you enough, Morna. There's no need for me to make a trip into the city now, but would it be all right with you if we stay here tonight and leave in the morning?"

"Of course, lass. I wouldna have it any other way. I'm anxious to catch up with Mary, and I canna wait to hear her cries of excitement when we allow her to take a hot shower."

Chapter 5

Near Conall Castle

1646

The wind blew icy snow roughly into his face, and Hew could barely see the path in front of him. His fingers and nose burned from the pain of the harsh wind and bitter cold. With each step forward, his horse slowed his pace.

He didn't wish to stop for the night. He was so very close to the end of his journey, but he knew that his four-legged companion would not be able to go much further. He groaned inwardly at the thought of where he knew he must stop. Conall Castle, his sister's place of residence, was so close that he could make it out in the distance, its grandness evident even through the storm.

Hew knew it had been far too long since he'd paid a visit to Mary, nearly ten years by his count, possibly longer. He missed her, but he knew she would treat his arrival as a celebration. The thought of such attention caused him to cringe inwardly.

Still, there was hardly another choice. Bracing himself for the torture he knew was about to ensue, he leaned down close

23

to Greggory's ear whispering words of encouragement as he nudged the old horse to the right. "Just a wee bit further, lad. There shall be a fine stable and blankets to keep ye warm just ahead. I'm sorry to have taken ye out in such a storm. I shall see ye well fed tonight, old fellow."

* * *

Flames flickered in the stables, so Hew knew before he approached that someone was still at work within them. They were most likely preparing the horses for the evening, making sure they were properly tended to in the cold weather.

He rode straight into the stables before calling out to whomever worked inside. He knew enough of the Conalls' generosity to know that they would not protest to anyone seeking shelter for their horse on such a night.

Hew dismounted, quickly brushing the snow off of Greggory's coat, jumping at the sound of the voice in the stall at the end. "What sort of a fool would travel in this weather? 'Tis no so good for yer horse, sir. What be yer name?"

Hew's cheeks suddenly warmed. For a moment, he feared he would be unable to utter a word. He'd not spoken to another person in many moons. He swallowed, steeling himself and spoke boldly. "The fool's name is Hew. I apologize for the intrusion, but I must ask yer permission to allow me and me horse to rest here for the night. The poor lad willna be able to go much further."

A strong lad as tall as him, with long, shaggy blonde hair stepped out of the stall and smiled as he walked toward him. He knew the man must be the youngest Conall brother, Arran, but the lad had been much younger the last Hew had seen him.

"Aye, of course ye can. It would be a wretched man to turn away anyone in a storm such as this."

Hew continued to rub the sleeves of his covering over his horse's coast, doing his best to dry the animal. "Thank ye, sir. I shall help ye in the cleaning of the stables come morning in payment for yer kindness. Ye are Arran, are ye no?"

Arran reached for a blanket draped over the doors of one of the stalls and moved to help him in his efforts. "Nay, that willna be necessary. Aye, I am Arran. Should I know ye, sir?"

Hew shook his head as they worked alongside each other, warming and drying the beast. "Nay, I doona expect that ye would remember me, but I believe that ye know me sister, Mary. Is she still in service to yer family?"

The strapping lad next to him patted the horse gently on the backside before casting a rather surprised expression in his direction. "Nay, ye canna mean it? Ye're Mary's brother? Well, 'tis a pleasure to meet ye. And aye, we know Mary well, but I wouldna say she is in our service. This castle is more hers than me brother's."

Hew laughed, it seemed his sister had changed little over the years. "Aye, lad, that sounds verra much like she would have it. I dread the fuss she shall make over me arrival, but I feel I must make me presence here known to her. Where can I find her?"

Arran fidgeted uncomfortably. For a moment Hew worried that perhaps his sister was unwell, but the lad recovered quickly. "Well, it seems that she herself has gone on a bit of a journey, but doona worry about the weather, we know that she is quite safe and out of the storm. I shall let her explain to ye where it is that she has gone once she returns."

Hew didn't understand what the lad meant, but he wasn't disappointed to learn that he would be able to rest before reuniting with his sister. "Ah, well, I'm certain she will be pleased to tell me all about it. She used to talk a great deal. I doona imagine that has changed."

Arran laughed and motioned at him to lead his horse into one of the empty stalls. "Nay, sir, she hasna changed. She's talked a lot for all the time that I've known her. Now, let us get yer horse settled, and ye shall follow me inside so that ye can have a room of yer own."

Hew stiffened and stopped moving forward. He would not be comfortable staying inside the castle. It was not where he belonged. He'd rather stay in the stables, with only the horses for company. "Nay, lad, I shall stay here with the horses. It would no be proper for me to accompany ye inside."

Arran insisted. "Nay proper me arse. I willna be letting ye stay out here in this weather. If Mary learned I'd done so, she'd kill me herself, I'm certain."

Hew didn't wish to be impolite to his host, but it was something he knew he had to insist on. He wouldn't sleep a wink in the presence of so many people. "I doona wish to offend ye, lad, but I simply canna stay in the castle. If ye willna allow me to remain out here, I'm afraid that Greggory and I will have to be on our way and take our chance with the snow."

Guilt filled Hew at the look of shock on Arran's face. If only the thought of company didn't paralyze him so.

"Nay, lad, please doona leave in this storm. Mary would rather me allow ye to sleep in the stables, I'm certain. But perhaps, I can provide ye with something a little more comfortable than stable floors.

"Truly, lad, 'tis no trouble for me to stay here. I've slept in worse many times before."

Arran shook his head as he draped Hew's horse with coverings. "Just listen to me before ye say nay to it. We have a cottage no far from here. 'Tis empty, no one stays there, and ye are welcome to stay there if ye wish. Ye can build ye a fire, and there is a proper bed. Please, sir, at least stay there."

Hew couldn't deny how pleasurable a warm fire and a soft bed sounded to him. As long as it was truly separate from the castle as the lad said, he thought he could find rest for the night there. "Aye, lad. I shall gladly stay in yer cottage. I'm sorry to be a bother to ye. I appreciate yer kindness."

Arran clasped him tightly on the shoulder. "Nay, sir, 'tis no trouble. I apologize for saying so, but ye're rather a strange fellow, are ye no?"

Hew laughed at the truthfulness in Arran's words as the young Conall showed him the way to the tiny cottage. "Aye, lad, that I am, verra strange indeed."

Chapter 6

Getting back to the seventeenth century was mildly tricky, but we managed. Because we brought with us two boxes of belongings and the precious vial I hoped would provide Bri with much relief once she went into labor, we were forced to sit on the floor of the spell room while we balanced the boxes in our laps. We chanted the words aloud together and reached over our boxes to link hands right before the spell began to work.

When we arrived back, we nursed our aching heads for a few short moments and then made our way up to the kitchen where we could hear Bri and her lookalike sister-in-law, Blaire, working together.

"We're back! What are you two girlies up to?" I sat the box I carried down just past the doorway and went to give both of the girls a quick hug, lingering an extra second so that I could press my hands against Bri's stomach to see if my grandbaby would give me a quick kick. For the moment, it seemed the infant slept soundly.

"Trying to cook, but it isn't going so well. Eoin and Arran will be thrilled that you're home, Mary. They're convinced that if they have to go another day with us as cooks, they shall starve to death." Bri winked at Mary and then bobbed her head in the direction of the box. "What did you get?"

I grabbed her hand and anxiously dragged her over so that I could reveal all of the precious goodies we'd returned with. "Morna knew what I wanted. She gathered up our ornament box. Isn't it wonderful?"

Bri moved to her knees instantly, her belly getting in the way, but I knew nothing would keep her from rummaging through the boxes. Each item was as special to her as it was to me. "Oh, Mom. You're joking! This is amazing, truly."

"Yes, it is, dear. She gathered a few other items for us as well, but I'm going to wait until later to show those to you. It can just be a surprise for everyone." I placed my hand on her shoulder as I squatted down next to her as we lifted each tiny memory out of the box.

Blaire walked across the room to stand next to us. "The storm has slowed a bit. 'Tis still impossible to go too far from the main building, but nay much is falling right now. Mayhap we should all go out together and find a tree to cut down for the decorations."

Bri leapt to her feet with more energy than I'd seen her exert in the last two months. "Yes, that's a perfect idea. I'll get Eoin. Blaire, you find Arran. Mom and Mary, go get Kip and meet us out back. Stat!"

She scurried off quickly, Blaire following suit. Mary and I laughed together, walking out of the kitchen so that we could prepare for our outing.

* * *

29

Both girls had apparently already decided that we would go tree hunting today if we returned from Morna's. The gathering of everyone went entirely too smoothly, as if they all waited on pins and needles for us to get home. The excitement of Christmas was starting to move through our merry little group.

The snow was beautiful, covering every inch of the castle grounds. I found myself wishing more than once that I'd enlisted Morna to cast us all a pair of sturdy snow boots as well, but we were all having such a wonderful time, none of us thought much about our ice-cold toes.

It took us some time before we found a tree that everyone could agree on. Many that held the perfect shape proved far too large. Some of perfect size were not the right shape. Eventually, the perfect tree stood before us. While Eoin, Arran, and Mary's husband, Kip, worked at chopping it down, all of us girls stood huddled together watching.

The landscape remained silent, save for the crack against the wood as the men took their turns driving the ax into its base. For a moment, I thought I'd imagined the soft whining sound coming from somewhere behind me, but as I listened I felt certain that I had not.

An animal, of that much I was sure, and a young one at that, made the noise. I couldn't tell what kind of creature it might be. My heart squeezed uncomfortably at the thought of anything so tiny and helpless being trapped out here in the snow.

Afraid that too many people approaching would cause it fear, I slowly crept away from the group and went off in search of the soft whine.

*   *   *

Hew stepped out in front of the small cottage, frowning as he looked out over the landscape drenched in snow. He'd hoped very much that he would be able to leave today, but it would be impossible. Even though snow no longer fell, he feared his horse might break a leg if he forced him to trudge through snow so deep.

He threw his arms up above him stretching and groaning at his frustration. In response to the noise he uttered from his throat, something whined not far from him. Compassion compelled him to go in search of the creature.

Turning, he draped himself in thick coverings. The chill from his ride yesterday still set deep within his bones. Grunting, he took off in the direction of the noise. He stepped only a few trees away from the cottage before he caught the dark, whimpering ball of fur at the base of the tree.

Hew bent, picking up the puppy gently as it shivered uncontrollably in his large hands. He wrapped the pup up in his own furs, rubbing his hands back and forth over the small creature to warm it. It was a miracle the creature still lived, for it must have spent the previous night out in the storm as well.

He held it closely to his chest, waiting for the puppy to stop trembling. When he felt its warm tongue start to lap at the inside of his fingers, he knew the pup was only cold, not injured. He uncovered the tiny animal, smiling as he took in its handsome features.

31

Hew raised him to check the gender and, finding him a boy, sat him back into the cradle of his hand. The dog was fluffy with thick hair that made him look much bigger than he seemed. Dark hair covered his back but a beautiful mixture of spots of gray, brown, and black fur covered his chest and feet. Warm brown eyes oozed kindness out of them. Small patches of light brown hair sat above his eyes, standing out on his black head, giving the illusion of brows.

"Why, ye are a handsome pup, are ye no?" He pulled the creature in close to him once more, reaching down to pick the clumps of icy snow from between the pup's paws. He stilled when another small whine caught his attention near him. "Ach, it seems that ye have another wee friend close to ye. Let's go find him together."

* * *

It had not taken me long to find the source of the noise. If not for the weak bark that the creature let out as I approached him, I would have probably stepped right on top of him, the white of his fur matching the snow.

The puppy lay hidden, only his black nose and mouth sticking up out of the drift, quite close to the Conalls' small cottage. I gasped when I saw him, quickly reaching down to snatch him out of his icy home as I brushed the snow off of him with my bare hands. "Oh you poor thing!"

The creature responded with another small bark. Once he was free of the snow, I lifted him, examining his coloring. His hair was straight but full. Beautiful, but the kind of dog I was sure would shed easily. White fur covered most of his body, but his backside was black. With the exception of his white mouth and snout, each side of his face and both ears were black, too.

I'd expected the creature to squirm in my grasp but, once he became warm, he collapsed relaxing completely, his small legs dangling on each side of my arm. I grinned as I pulled him in close. I hoped very much that Eoin would not object to having a dog in the castle because the pup would come with me regardless.

A voice behind me caused me to jump, jerking my arm so that the puppy came awake, groaning in displeasure.

"Ah, I thought I heard another one making noise. Seems our two little friends must be brothers, aye?"

I turned around to face the most handsome man I had ever seen.

Chapter 7

"Oh my, you scared me. Hello there." I lifted my knees high as I moved closer to him. I didn't miss the strange expression that crossed his face when he heard the way I spoke. Everyone in this time did that.

"'Ello to ye too, lass. I apologize for frightening ye. 'Twas no my intention. I heard this wee lad, no far from the one ye hold in yer hands. I still heard whining so I knew there must be another close." He pointed to the black squirmy ball in his hands. The pup he held was far less content to be held than the one lying like broccoli in my arms.

I stood close to the man now and extended my hand to touch the wiggly pup he held. The dog's fur felt soft like baby hair. As I rubbed him, the man reached his hand to rub the pup I held.

"They are both fine looking pups, are they no?"

I nodded as we both pulled our hands away. "Yes, beautiful dogs. Look at the markings above their eyes. They look quite different, but they must be out of the same litter."

"Aye, lass, I believe ye are right. They are the same size and age. Forgive me, miss. Me manners are no what they should be. Me name is Hew. To whom do I find meself speaking to?"

34

I reached out to shake his hand. My stomach fluttered as he grabbed my fingertips, briefly touching them to his lips. I was far too old to have such a reaction to a man, but God he was a beautiful being. "Um…" I faltered and blushed, totally out of character from my normally over-confident, over-flirty self. "Um…Adelle. My name is Adelle."

I guessed he was only a few years older than me, if not the same age. Thick, dark, wavy curls, only lightly sprinkled with salt, covered his head. He kept it cropped short unlike many men in this time who wore theirs longer. I preferred that. I didn't see the appeal in being with a man who had more hair on his head than I do.

Tall, with broad shoulders, every inch of him was covered, I had a feeling he would not be soft like many men our age. He worked hard. It was evident in the tone of his skin and the light crease of wrinkles across his brow. A light shadow of a beard only added to the manliness he exuded.

The way he stood awkwardly after I told him my name hinted at shyness. Now that we'd introduced ourselves to one another, he seemed uncertain of how to continue the conversation.

I had to shake my head to recover, yanking my stare away from the deep green abysses of his eyes. "Um…are you from around here? Do you live in the village?"

He bent his head to glance at his puppy, finally no longer squirming as it slept in his arms. "Nay, lass. I doona live anywhere near here. I'm on me way elsewhere but had to stop here due to the storm. I am staying in this cottage here," he pointed behind him. "The Conalls were kind enough to grant me refuge from the snow. Me sister lives with them and works in the castle."

Only one woman worked for the Conalls and actually lived in the castle beside myself, but there was no possible way the god that stood before me could be the brother Mary had been talking about. "You wouldn't be speaking of Mary, would you? Your sister is someone else, yes?"

Hew's eyes sparked a brilliant green, lighting flutters in my stomach once more. "Aye, lass, 'tis Mary that I speak of. Do ye know her then?"

Stunned, I had based my mental image of Mary's brother based on her appearance and envisioned a short, round, aging bald man who talked loudly. This man was none of those things. His voice was deep, but he spoke quietly and said nothing more than required by the conversation. "Yes, I know Mary quite well. She's just around the corner here, along with everyone else from the castle. We've been cutting a tree down for Christmas. Does she know that you're here? Mary and I were away yesterday, we only just returned this morning."

He shook his head. "I doona know if she is aware of me presence yet, but I guess 'tis time that she is. Will ye lead the way there for me, lass?"

"Of course." I turned and waved so that he would follow me. I felt self-conscious with my back exposed to him. With every step, I damned myself for pinning my hair up into a hideous bun before we trekked out into the snow.

The group saw me first, and Mary immediately tore into me for stepping away from their company. "Adelle, what is the matter with ye? Why did ye run off without telling us where ye'd gone? Ye could have frozen to death…"

She paused when she caught sight of her brother and moved her short, stumpy legs faster than I'd have ever thought possible as she charged through the snow to throw herself into his arms.

Hew let out a puff of air as she squeezed him and then pushed her away as gently as he could. "Be careful, Mary. Ye shall squish the wee pup I hold in me arms."

Mary glanced briefly down at the sleeping dog but was un-phased by the adorable bundle. Bri and Blaire, on the other hand, immediately went to snatch the pups from each of our arms.

"What are ye doing here, Hew? I havena seen ye in years. God, ye look good, brother!" Once Hew was free of the puppy, Mary threw her arms around him again.

"I was on me way to Mae's grave, but the storm caused me to seek shelter here. I only arrived last evening."

The sadness I'd seen earlier in Mary briefly crossed her face, and I wondered greatly about the identity of Mae. The pain showed only for a moment before Mary whirled away from her brother to face the crowd of all of us watching curiously.

"I see, and which one of ye knew he was here and dinna tell me the second I arrived with Adelle this morning?"

Bri, Blaire, Eoin, and Kip all looked back and forth at each other, clearly in the dark, while Arran glanced sheepishly at the ground. Eventually, he spoke up. "'Twas I, Mary. I apologize. I'm a fool. I got so caught up in the lasses' excitement over finding a tree that I forgot to tell ye."

I thought for a moment she would march through the snow and smack him, but her happiness at seeing her brother seemed to override her annoyance at not learning of his presence until now.

"Shame on ye, Arran, but 'tis no matter now. Why doona the rest of ye go on back to the castle with the tree? I shall join ye shortly after I spend some time speaking with me brother, aye?"

Eoin spoke as he directed us all back to the castle. "Aye, Mary. Spend as much time as ye wish. I suppose we willna starve from only one more night of Bri and Blaire's cooking. Yer brother is welcome to dine with us, but if ye wish to spend some time alone together, I can bring ye food later this evening."

I was surprised when Hew responded to Eoin instantly. "I would be much obliged to ye if ye would allow us to dine in the cottage. I shall repay yer kindness in some way."

He obviously didn't want to dine with everyone. Not that I could blame him. We were a bit much to take. Still, his quick rejection seemed a little odd. He walked over to Blaire who was holding his new puppy. After she extended it in his direction, he and Mary turned to make their way back to the cottage.

* * *

As we returned the short distance back to the castle, both Bri and Blaire squeezed in tight on either side of me while I balanced my puppy in between my open palms. The girls leaned in close so that they could hear the other's whispers.

"Mom, holy cow, would you ever have thought Mary's brother would look like that?" Bri nudged my side playfully.

I smiled, laughing as I shook my head. I leaned into her, nudging her back. "No, not in a million years would I have expected that."

"Ye did find him a handsome lad, aye Adelle?" Blaire spoke next, her voice as quiet and excited as Bri's.

"Oh yes, very much so. He's quite striking. Why do you ask?" He was married, of course. All the good ones were.

"He's a bit of a hermit from what Eoin and Arran told us. His wife died decades ago, and he lives all alone far away from anyone else. Seems a bit crazy to me, but Eoin seems to think he's just shy. Regardless, does it matter if he's crazy when he looks that good?"

I laughed loudly, garnering questioning glances from the three men walking in front of us. Bri liked to think she was my polar opposite, but she was more like her Mama than she wanted to admit. "Well, it does matter a bit, yes, but I don't think he's crazy." We were approaching the castle. "Let's not gossip anymore now, the boys will give me a hard time. I'm going to find some food for this little one to eat."

Once inside, the girls dispersed, and I carried the sleeping pup down into the kitchen while I thought on what I'd just learned about our new visitor. He was unmarried then.

And I was not displeased to hear it.

Chapter 8

All was abuzz within the confines of Conall Castle the next day. It was decorating day and, with the visitation of her brother, Mary's spirits rose as high as I'd ever seen them. As a result, everyone else in the castle couldn't help but be merry as well.

I'd not expected us to put the tree in the castle's main entrance. I worried that with the modern ornaments we planned to put on the tree, it might raise suspicions of other castle workers. I could not have been more surprised when I made my way down in the morning to find that Eoin, Arran, and Kip had placed the tree there.

"Do you not think it would be best if we set up the tree in the basement? I won't be able to hang the ornaments on it otherwise, right?"

"Aye, ye will. Feel free to hang anything that we wish from the tree. I willna have us hiding our celebrations. All who work within the castle know of Morna's legacy and her spells." Eoin walked up to me and bent to briefly kiss me on the cheek. "Good morning, Adelle."

I smiled, so very pleased that my daughter had found such a wonderful man. "Oh great, that's wonderful. It will look beautiful in the corner there, next to the grand fireplace."

41

"Aye, it will. Look." Eoin pointed to the staircase behind me. "Here come the other lassies. Let us eat and then we will begin the festivity of decorating."

* * *

Over breakfast, I couldn't help but notice Hew's absence from the table once again. I was fairly sure he hadn't left already. The snow still had not melted enough for travel, and there was little way for him to get food in the cottage without someone bringing it to him. I didn't understand why he seemed so set against joining us in the castle. I leaned over to Mary to ask her about it. "Why won't your brother join us here to eat? He knows that he's welcome, doesn't he?"

Mary pulled one corner of her mouth to the side uncomfortably before casting sad eyes in my direction. "Aye, he knows it, but he insists on being alone."

"Why is that?" I looked down at my food so that my interest wouldn't seem too eager.

"He's painfully shy. He's spent so much time alone, I'm afraid he doesna know how to be around other people any more."

That seemed a hard concept for me to grasp. I loved spending every second in the company of others. It was unhealthy for someone to live in such a way. It might be one thing for a person to spend time alone by their own choice, but another to feel that they were prevented from joining others due to shyness. "Well, the only way to get less shy is to practice. Will you see him this morning?"

Mary nodded. "Aye, I shall bring him something to eat as soon as we finish here before we begin decorating."

"Ask him to join us and help in the decorations. It's going to be a lot of fun. Insist on it, Mary. You can be very persuasive."

Mary chuckled but shook her head. "That may be true with many people, Adelle, but nay with me brother. I can insist until the stars have risen, and it will no persuade him to do something he doesna wish to do."

I frowned. I didn't like the thought of Hew being all alone in the cottage while the rest of us spent a joyous day decorating. "Well, will you ask him at least?"

Mary stood, covering a plate to take to her brother. "Aye, lass. I'll ask him."

* * *

Perhaps he'd been too short with his sister. It wasn't unreasonable for her to wish that he would spend some time with her by joining in the festivities. He would make time to see her later, when she was alone, but his shyness would have done nothing but dampen the spirits of everyone else.

Hew no longer knew how to behave comfortably in front of anyone, let alone an entire family of people who evidently were quite close to one another. He'd managed well enough when he'd bumped into Adelle the day he'd found the pup now sleeping at his feet, but that was an unusual occurrence. He would be certain to make an effort to spend a little more time with his sister before he left.

He reached down to rub on the sleeping pup, thinking back on the strangest thing his sister had told him. She'd said more than once that Adelle had insisted that he come to the castle and help them with the decorations. Why would the lass desire such a thing?

She must feel sorry for him. Any other possibility seemed too unrealistic for him to think of. There'd only been one woman fancy him in his whole life. It wouldn't make sense for another lass to decide to do so now.

Would it?

Chapter 9

I waited until all of the men started trimming the tree, working it into the perfect shape, before I snuck away to grab the surprise I had in store for all of them.

Mary's trip to see her brother had been quick. When she arrived back at the castle without Hew, I knew he had rejected her invitation to join us. I couldn't help the small pang of sadness that lodged itself in my chest, but I did my best to dismiss it. I hardly knew the man after all. What did I care if he chose to be such a fuddy duddy?

Blaire had already helped Bri carry the large box of ornaments upstairs, so while the men shaved away at the tree and the girls marveled at each ornament as they pulled them out of the box, I went down to the basement once more.

Opening the box, I pulled out the large boombox, flipping it over so that I could install a fresh set of batteries. Placing the cd player under one arm and a stack of CDs under the other, I made my way upstairs.

Once I got into the great room, I walked with my back toward them to shield the contents in my arms and sat the player discreetly next to the fire, hidden away behind a large seat. I thought best to select a classical Christmas mix first. I was afraid anything too modern would frighten the bejeezus out of Arran and Kip, both of whom had never made a trip through time.

I started it with the volume low so that it played just loud enough to cause everyone in the room to glance around as if they were imagining the sounds in their heads. Slowly, I increased the intensity of the sound until Kip threw both his hands to his ears and looked up to the ceiling in horror.

"What in the name o' God is that? I've told all of ye, I doona like the magic that seems to go on in this place. Make it stop."

Mary laughed and walked over to grab her husband's wrists as she pried his hands away from his head. "Doona be such a fool, Kip. 'Tis no magic, only a music maker we brought back from our journey. Do ye no think it sounds lovely?"

Kip didn't answer right away. Instead, Arran spoke up, "I've never heard such beautiful noise in me life. Leave it be, 'tis magical."

Eventually, Kip surrendered and joined in with the humming and singing as we spent the day turning Conall Castle into a Christmas wonderland. The tree didn't take all that long. Then Mary took us girls downstairs to make garland and wreaths to hang up around the castle.

Though hard work, twisting the leaves and branches into some semblance of something that would please the eye, Mary, Blaire, and Bri took to it quite well. All of my projects were an undisputable disaster.

I'd not been a crafty woman in the twenty-first century, where craft stores within a three-block radius sold glues and tools to help you. Without such conveniences, it was pure misery for me to even try.

After three failed wreaths and a string of garland only the *Grinch* would appreciate, I was taken off craft duty and given the measly task of hanging the mistletoe that Bri had created above the entryway into the dining hall.

Mary thought the tradition of mistletoe to be a brilliant idea. "Ye mean that if I can somehow trick Kip into standing beneath the doorway with me, he will be forced to kiss me? Why, I shall stand there all day and wait for him to pass through! I doona believe the old bugger will even remember what part of yer body that ye use to kiss, 'tis been so long since he's done so."

I laughed but, as I did so, Mary's brother crossed my mind once more. I imagined if what Bri and Blaire thought they knew about Hew was true, it had been quite some time since he'd been kissed as well. For some reason, I wished to be the person to change that for him. "Mary, would ye mind if I brought Hew some food to eat after the evening meal?"

She clucked her tongue at me, knowingly. "Ach, I knew there was a reason ye wished me to ask Hew to help with the decorations. Ye have taken a liking to him then, have ye?'

I reddened, something that seemed to be happening much more frequently. I didn't like it one bit. "Well, what if I have?"

Mary laughed and looked down to concentrate on the bunch of stems in her hand. "Nothing, dear. It has been far too long since Hew has shared his company with another. Please, I would love for ye to take him his food. I doona like getting out in the snow anyway."

"Will he be angry, do you think? I don't want to upset him. I just thought perhaps I could bring some of the decorations that we didn't use, and I could leave them for him to set up at the cottage. It would give him something to do and, with the snow still piled up, I don't think he will be leaving us anytime soon."

"Right ye are, lass, and he willna be angry at all. He's a kind man, although I'll admit that he is slow to warm. But once ye reach the man he really is, behind his shyness, why..." she paused smiling down at her wreath, "he's a man worth getting to know."

Chapter 10

The cottage stood silent in front of me. For a moment I feared he'd already gone to sleep for the evening, but the puppy I cradled underneath my arm let out a high-pitched yelp. Within seconds, the door to the cottage flew open.

"Ach, evening, Adelle. I feared for a moment there was a third pup who had found his way out of the snow, but I see 'tis only yer little fellow."

"Ah, yes." I paused and waved Arran away now that he'd dragged the small tree we'd just cut down in front of the cottage and helped me carry the food and decorations close to the door. "Thank you, Arran. I'll make it up to you somehow."

Arran called back to me over his shoulder as he turned and made his way through the darkness, leaving Hew and I alone. "Nay, there is no need, Adelle. Be careful on yer way back to the castle."

I'd instructed him to leave as soon as he dropped off all of the items. I wanted a chance to be alone with the quiet, strange man, and I didn't want to chance that he would ask Arran to stick around as well.

Not that I should've been concerned. With the look of surprise on Hew's face, I wondered if I would even be invited inside. I lifted up the basket of food I held in my left hand as I set my pup down on the ground. He immediately ran inside the cottage to join his brother. "Um...Mary was busy so I told her I would bring you something to eat. I hope you don't mind. I also," I pointed to the items behind me, "brought some decorations. We had some left over from today, and I thought it would give you something to do, ya know, if you wanted to decorate the cottage for Christmas."

He scrunched his brows together. I couldn't tell if he was just confused or disgusted. I'd not given much thought to the fact that he was a man and probably didn't give two flips about beautifying anything. I'd simply been trying to spread the cheer. "I...you don't have to take the decorations. I can come back with Arran in the morning and get them. But at least take the food. I'll just head back to the castle now." I squatted awkwardly, whistling to my pup to come, but to no avail. The two brothers wrestled playfully on the floor with no intention of ending their little games anytime soon.

Hew surprised me by reaching out to put his hand on my shoulder. "Nay, lass, I shall enjoy the decorations. Please, come inside."

He stepped aside to usher me in, and I immediately did so, running my hands up and down over my arms to warm myself.

"Come sit by the fire while I set the table. Surely ye are in no hurry to return to the castle. Why doona ye stay and eat with me? I'm sorry if I gave ye the feeling I wished for ye to leave. 'Twas simply that I was surprised by yer presence."

"Oh." I wanted to smack myself square in the forehead at my inability to speak like a grown woman in front of him. It was absolutely ridiculous. No man, not even Bri's father, had the ability to render me speechless so completely.

"Did ye already eat, lass? If so, I shall wait until after ye have gone. Perhaps ye can at least warm yerself by the fire for a little while, aye?"

For someone so shy, he tried. I rewarded his efforts by appearing far less friendly than I actually was. I loved to talk and, by golly, I intended to do so. I sat my mind to acting human again before I opened my mouth. "No. I haven't eaten."

He stood and moved to the small table, laying out the spread I'd brought for him. "Come and join me, lass."

* * *

We ate quietly. While I searched my mind for ideas of what I could speak to him about, each time I stopped myself short. He could sense my hesitation as sometimes I even uttered a syllable only to then stop talking. He took pity on me by speaking himself. "I apologize for the way I behaved when I opened the door. I am verra much accustomed to being all alone. Although I am a visitor here, visitors of me own are verra unexpected. Might I tell ye something?"

I nodded. "Of course."

"'It occurred to me that perhaps ye keep stopping yerself from speaking because ye are worried that I might notice the odd way in which ye speak."

That had nothing to do with it, but I didn't want to object when he obviously put so much thought into it. Instead, I remained silent and waited for him to continue. He did so shortly.

"I confess that I did take note of it when I first met ye, but 'twas only after Mary told me yer story about where and when ye came from that I understood. So doona worry, lass, I willna judge the way ye speak. I'm no so good at speaking with others meself."

Surprised by his words, I smiled before speaking. Mary hadn't lied. Her brother was a kind man. "How is it that you seem to have believed what Mary told you so easily? It is hard for even those of us who have experienced Morna's magic to accept it."

"Ach, ye have found yer voice. I am glad for it." He smiled slightly.

If I'd been standing, I expect my knees would have grown weak at the beauty of it.

"I knew Morna when I was a child, and I grew up hearing stories of her powers. I know me sister well enough to know that she wouldna lie to me about such a matter. Besides, life is such that many things happen that we canna explain how or why they do. It must have been quite a change for ye to come here, aye?"

Our food was now gone, and I knew I would be expected to take my leave soon. "Yes, it was, but one I welcomed. With my daughter being here, there's nowhere else I'd rather be, and I love it here very much." I stood, pushing my chair in before walking to the door. "Why don't I help you carry these things in then I'll leave you be for the evening."

The same unreadable look that had crossed his face earlier resurfaced, and I was afraid I'd somehow upset him. He cast his palm out in the direction of the empty room. "Are ye no going to stay and help me? It seems ye have brought enough to decorate an entire village, and I havena celebrated the holiday since I was a small child. I'm afraid I shallna know what to do with all of it on me own."

I beamed and stepped out into the darkness so he wouldn't see my reddened face. "Yes, I would love to."

For someone that didn't like the company of others, he seemed to be in no hurry to rid himself of mine.

* * *

The lass must still carry Morna's magic with her for her to have such an effect on him. He'd been surprised by her slim presence at the door but was pleased to see her, blonde hair blowing wildly in the breeze, as she quickly sent Arran away. She wanted to be alone with him. While he wasn't sure why, the thought made something deep within him warm for the first time in ages.

At first, Adelle had seemed more nervous even than he felt, and it somehow helped to calm his nerves in the beauty's presence. In fact, he felt very much himself with her and talked as freely as he did with anyone.

The lass' shyness had not lasted long. After he'd asked her to stay and help him with the decorations, she'd talked with him at length, telling him grand stories of all that had happened at Conall Castle within the last months. Hew found himself for the first time wishing he had not stayed away from his homeland for so long.

When all that Adelle had brought him was set just as the lass would have it, he walked her back to the castle, his heart more sad than he would allow himself to admit that their evening together had come to an end.

"Thank you for allowing me to interrupt your evening. I hope I wasn't too much of a bother."

The lass was mad if she was unable to see how much he had enjoyed her company, but he suspected his feelings that he always kept locked deep away within him did not show clearly on his face as he sometimes wished they would.

He stared directly into her green eyes, so vibrant and alive that he couldn't help but realize how little he'd allowed himself to truly live for far too many years. She was the most beautiful woman he had ever seen, her pale face pink from standing out the cold. He wanted to do nothing more than warm them with the touch of his lips.

"Nay, lass, ye were no a bother at all. I had a wonderful time."

Mustering all the courage he had left in him for the evening, he quickly leaned in to kiss her on her cheek. Turning before she could see his reaction, he marched back into the darkness, his heart beating faster than it had in decades.

Chapter 11

I left my bedchamber early the next morning to join everyone in the dining hall for breakfast, still high on the endorphins that had surged through me at the touch of Hew's lips on my cheek the night before. I reminded myself repeatedly that it had only been the cheek, but it did nothing to push the giddy flurries away. What would I have done if he'd given me a proper kiss?

Visions of me pouncing him in the middle of the snow, begging him to take me right up against the castle wall flashed through my mind, and I shook my head in disgust. I was going to be a grandmother for goodness sakes.

But honestly, who was I kidding? If I expected that to turn me into a respectable, 'normal' woman in her fifties, I was sure to be disappointed. I'd always been a bit young on the inside, immature some would say, and I didn't have hope that that would change any time soon. I'd given up on it ages before.

I walked into the dining hall, and I was sure my eyes widened in surprise at seeing Hew sitting at the table alongside everyone else. Doing my best to hide my shock, I sat at my usual place at the table and turned to listen to Eoin, who was addressing the table.

"Are ye finished with yer meal, lads? If so, let us be on our way. I'm no so inclined to leave Bri's side, but she was verra insistent that we make this trip."

Bri nodded and waved him off, patting her stomach with her other hand. "Yes, I was. Be gone, all of you, and have a wonderful time. The baby seems content where it is. I'm certain it will be days until the birth."

"Where are you going?" I'd obviously missed the front of this conversation, but regardless, I was not one willing to be left out of the loop.

Bri responded from across the table. "Since Christmas Eve is only days away, the men are leaving us for a few days to go on a hunt. Hew has agreed to stay with us until after the holiday. He's going to help them on the hunt. Mary says he is a fine shot with an arrow."

"Wonderful. Are you boys certain you trust us to have free run of the castle while you're away?"

Eoin laughed as the other men rose from their places at the table. "Oh Adelle, ye all have free run as it is now, do ye no?"

I had nothing to say to that. He was right. We most certainly all did exactly as we wished. Headstrong women filled Conall Castle.

As they prepared to leave, Hew walked from around the table to stand at my side, carrying his puppy that had been hidden underneath the table at his feet.

"Will ye watch over him for me while I am away, lass?" He sat him next to my pup, and they instantly began gnawing at each other's faces playfully. "They seem quite attached to one another."

I grinned, nodding emphatically. I was so pleased and surprised to see that he'd decided to join the men on their hunt. "Of course. I'll take excellent care of him."

"Aye, I'm sure ye will, lass."

He turned and left without bidding farewell to anyone else in the room, even Mary, and I could almost see the steam coming from her ears.

* * *

"What did ye do to him last night, Adelle? Ye are the hussy I always thought ye were, are ye no? Why, ye have gone and soiled me brother the first evening ye spend alone with him!"

Mary had waited all of five seconds after the men had left the dining hall to tear into me, and my mouth fell open in response to her attack. "What? Are you mad? Of course I didn't! But even if I had, he wouldn't have been 'soiled.' He was married once before, was he not? I didn't do anything to him, save talk his ear off. He was very kind to put up with my presence."

I watched as Mary's face changed from one of anger to sheer surprise. "So ye swear to me then, ye dinna bed him?"

Whatever anger that had faded from Mary had moved into me. "Mary, if I weren't afraid you would knock me flat onto

57

my ass, I'd be half tempted to throttle you right now. It is absolutely none of your business what I did with your brother."

"So ye did then?"

Bri and Blaire glanced nervously at one another, and I could tell they wondered if they must stand in between us to keep us from attempting to strangle one another. Both of us needed to calm down. "No, I did no such thing, Mary."

"Oh." Mary stood and walked around the room as if trying to accept my words as truth.

"Oh, is right. You should feel mighty ashamed of yourself for assuming such a thing." I leaned back in my chair, crossing my arms to show my frustration.

"Mom, in Mary's defense, Hew is her brother, and it's not as if what she accused you of would be completely unheard of with you."

I shot Bri a look that must have been frightening for she sank down into her chair and didn't say another word as we all waited for Mary to say something else.

Eventually, she exhaled exaggeratedly and moved to resume her seat at the table. "Well, if ye dinna bed him, me brother must fancy the oddest of women, because he's mighty taken with ye."

"Why do you say that?" My face warmed, and I reached up to fan myself. At least at this age, I could pass any sudden redness off to hormones.

"I all but begged him to join us as ye bid me to do yesterday, and he would no come. He spends one evening in yer company, and he shows up at the castle this morning without being asked. He's always welcome o'course, but 'tis shocking behavior from him, Adelle. He even suggested the hunt. He went to Eoin early this morning and told him that he thought he'd found some great places for hunting on his way here."

"Is that so?" I looked down at myself. Damn the lack of air conditioning in this century.

Bri smiled and pointed at my face. "Mom, you're blushing. You like him, don't you?"

She skated on thin ice this morning. "Yes, I do but I am not blushing. I'm far too old to blush. It's just very warm in here is all. I think I'm having a hot flash."

Blaire spoke up, ganging up on me with Bri. "Nay, Adelle. 'Tis no warm in here at all. I doona believe ye are having a flash of warmth. I think Bri is right, ye're blushing."

"Why don't the two of you just bugger off?" I stood and left the dining hall so that I could find some cold water to splash on my face.

Chapter 12

They'd stayed close to the castle, finding shelter for them and their horses in the village, but the hunt had done them all good. Hew was accustomed to spending his days working hard on his land. He didn't like being cooped up in the confines of the small cottage each day.

He'd wanted to learn more about Adelle while away but had hoped he would be able to keep his growing feelings for her a secret. He'd been completely unsuccessful. It seemed all of the men had assumed his sudden eagerness to join in the castle activities had something to do with her.

As they made their way to their rooms in the inn they'd rented for the evening, Arran nudged him in the ribs as if they'd known one another forever. "Did ye enjoy Adelle's company last night? Ye must have, for I know I was unable to convince ye to step inside the castle walls."

Hew couldn't lie to him. Just the thought of her made something deep within his chest hum with an excitement he'd thought himself no longer capable of feeling. "Aye, lad. I verra much enjoyed the time we spent together."

"And ye find her a bonny looking lass, do ye no?"

The lad was forward, but Hew expected it was how he was with everyone. Arran didn't seem the kind of man to mince his words no matter who he found himself in the company of. "Aye, she's as beautiful a lass as I ever have seen. Do ye know her well, Arran?"

"Aye. I've spent much of the last year with her. She's wonderful, a little more forthright with her words than most lasses, but I wouldna have her any other way. Mary, Blaire, and Bri are much the same way, so perhaps that is why I doona mind her so much. I find fiery lasses to be the best company."

"Nay, I doona mind it either. Me wife was verra much like that. She always said whatever came to her mind. 'Twas a treasure to be with a woman I never had to wonder what she was thinking." Hew smiled, slightly surprised at himself. It was the first time he'd spoken of his wife in years that sadness hadn't crept into his heart.

"Well, ye never have to wonder what Adelle is thinking, 'tis certain. Ye shall be joining us for the meal on Christmas Eve, aye? It would disappoint her if ye dinna, and I can tell by the sparkle in yer eye when ye speak of her that ye doona wish to do that."

The last thing he wanted to do was upset Adelle in anyway. He was slowly beginning to want to do nothing more than please her. "Aye, lad, I'll be there. Ye are right, I doona wish to disappoint her at all."

* * *

The men arrived back at the castle midday on Christmas Eve. The prizes of the hunt were such that I was immediately forced to join Mary in the kitchen so that we could get to work preparing the meat. Bri and Blaire somehow evaded the kitchen. I suspected they were both spending private moments with their husbands, who they'd not seen for a whole three days.

It seemed a bit ridiculous to me that such a short period of separation seemed to cause them both such distress, but the truth was I was a little envious of the relationships they had found. I'd never had that with Bri's father. We both celebrated at the absence of the other. Even after our divorce, I'd never dated anyone long enough to allow my feelings to get all that strong.

By the time all of the food was prepared, everyone but Mary and I sat waiting anxiously in the dining hall, ready to devour the feast that was about to be placed before them. I'd just stepped into the room when I tripped on the bottom of my dress, causing me to slip forward.

I was certain I would land on the floor, spilling the precious bread basket I held in my hands, but Hew's quick hands suddenly set me right. He'd jumped up to pull a piece of garland out of his curious puppy's mouth and had passed by just in time to keep me from my fall.

"Are ye all right, lass? Mary would kill ye if ye dropped the food."

"Yes, she most certainly would. Thank you." I looked up at him, instantly lost in the greenness of his eyes. He didn't let go of my forearms, and it took Arran's voice from the table to pull us away from our locked gazes.

"Look up. Ye have both found yerself beneath the mistletoe. Ye must kiss her, Hew. 'Tis bad luck if ye doona."

Our eyes met once more. I was certain he wouldn't kiss me. It had been much for him to kiss my cheek in private. This would be too much to ask of him.

He didn't glance away. Instead, leaning in close until his lips were just a hair's width from mine, he whispered, "It seems that I must. I willna have bad luck following ye, lass."

His lips pressed warm, soft, and shy. I melted into him, nearly winding my fingers up into his hair as the butterflies in my stomach coursed through every inch of my body. Mary's voice to the other side of us caused him to pull away from me.

"Well, now ye have gone and ruined it. Now that Kip has seen what that is for, I shall never be able to trap him beneath it."

Hew laughed but leaned into my ear after Mary passed by us, whispering so that no one but me could hear him. "I intend to finish that kiss later, lass."

I smiled and whispered back, not caring about the eyes focused on us. "I surely hope so."

Chapter 13

Christmas morning was all that I'd hoped it would be. Presents, a beautiful tree, a warm fire, and lots of love and laughter filled the castle. Together, we lit the candle to place in the window to light the way for strangers, a New Year's tradition Mary shared with us. I'd heard of the custom through my archaeological studies, but it became a treat to be an active participant in the ritual.

When Bri opened the baby blanket, she'd cried big fish tears that soon had all of the women, even Mary, blubbering like babies. The baby was to come any day now so I'd also wrapped up the vial Morna had sent with me. Bri's reaction was just what I had expected.

"Oh, thank God! I've been so terrified for weeks at the pain. I'd about made up my mind that I was not going to let the child come out. If the medicine came from Morna, it's certain to help, don't you think?"

I suspected she was getting her hopes up a little high. While I was sure it would help to dull her pain a little, the pain of childbirth was such that there was little chance of it being a pain- free experience. I didn't imagine that's what she wanted to hear, so I simply smiled and nodded. "Yes, I'm sure it will help."

Hew had joined us but remained standoffish. I assumed he didn't want to make any of us feel guilty for not having gifts for him. I did, however. It just wasn't quite ready yet, and I didn't want him to know until later. I would need to enlist Mary's help to finish it. I'd done a fantastic job of thoroughly screwing it up.

I walked over to him, gently reaching out to touch his arm. "Merry Christmas."

He smiled, reaching up to gently squeeze my hand. "Merry Christmas to ye as well, lass. It has been many years since I have been able to witness such a wonderful celebration, but now I believe I shall take me leave and return to the cottage for awhile."

"Oh, please don't. We all enjoy having you here. Do you feel uncomfortable?"

"Nay, lass. I am surprised to say that I am verra comfortable with all of ye. 'Tis only that I have something I'd like to give ye but 'tis no quite finished yet. Would ye stop by the cottage in a little while?"

I smiled, but panic rushed through me. "Yes, of course I will." I wasn't going to accept a gift from him unless I had something to give him in return. That meant I didn't have much time to convince Mary to help me fix the disaster I tried to sew together yesterday morning.

He smiled, squeezing my hand once more before he slipped away. As soon as I saw him gone, I crossed the room to yank Mary up from her chair.

"You have got to come help me, quick. I tried to make Hew something, but I've messed it all up. Now he's going to give me something, so I need you to repair my gift to him."

"Ach, I see how he is. He will give his hussy a gift but no his sister. Did I just hear ye say ye tried to sew something, Adelle?"

Mary looked at me begrudgingly but stood. I knew she would be happy to help. "Yes, I know. Horrible idea."

"Aye, lass," Mary laughed heartily. "Ye are a fool, but I'm so happy this Christmas morning, I doona mind telling ye that I love ye dearly. Now, let's go fix the mess ye've made. Me brother deserves a proper gift."

Chapter 14

I knocked on the door to the cottage with numb fingers and a red nose. It had started snowing once more, and the wind blew bitterly cold. He opened the door quickly, smiling wide.

"Come inside, lass. Ye and the pup both. 'Tis freezing outside."

A large fire burned from the hearth, making the room warm, almost toasty, inside. He was wearing less clothing than I'd ever seen him in. I had to swallow hard at the sight of seeing what I thought he would look like underneath his big coat the first day I'd met him. He wore long pants, his shirt thin linen exposing part of his chest. Chest hair poked out from the top.

Once I stood inside, he pulled me into a large hug. I breathed in deeply at the masculine scent of him as my face pressed flat against his chest. "I'm sorry it took me so long. I had to get Mary to help me finish your gift. I made quite a mess of it."

He crossed the room to grab a small box that sat in the windowsill next to the tree. "Ye doona need to give me a gift, lass."

"Well, same goes for you then. But, it seems that we both did anyway, so let's exchange them."

I didn't wait for him to give me mine before extending the two folded pieces of cloth I held in my hands. He took them, and after unfolding them, stared down at the odd pieces quizzically. "Thank ye, lass, but what exactly is it that I'm holding?"

I bent down and snatched up my puppy who snuggled next to his brother near the fire. Reaching out, I took one of the pieces from him and gently slipped it over the puppy's head, pushing each leg through the tiny holes.

He laughed loudly. "Did ye truly make a shirt for the pups? Is this a common thing where ye come from?"

I smiled. I knew he would find it silly, but there was no denying how precious both of them would look in their small, wool onesies. "Yes, I surely did. Not all that common, but a few crazy people like me do sometimes dress their dogs. You can't deny how cute they look."

He grinned picking up the other pup as he slipped the small creation over the animal. "Nay, lass, I canna deny it. They shall be the bonniest, most ridiculous-looking pups anywhere. It seems that our gifts will compliment one another."

"Oh yeah? How?"

He placed the box inside my hands. "Open it and see, lass. I hope that ye like them. It has been some time since I have carved anything."

I lifted the top of the wooden box gently. The box itself was exquisite, crafted by fine hands. I could only imagine how magnificent the contents inside the box would be. I lifted the small piece of cloth covering the items, and I had to choke back tears when I saw what lay inside.

Two wooden ornaments lay nestled within, each dangling from crimson ribbons, carved perfectly into the shape of dogs, puppies to be exact. Their resemblance to the pups snuggling at our feet was striking.

I'd not had a gift so touching in many years. It wasn't the ornaments themselves, although they were certainly impressive. The attention and thought that had gone into such a gift touched me deeply. He'd listened to me the night we'd decorated the cottage together and taken special note of my love for such objects.

His voice startled me from my gaze. "Do ye no like them, lass? I'm no so good at crafting wood as I once was. I'm a bit out of practice."

"No." I reached out to grab him firmly by the hand. "They're amazing, Hew, truly. I love them. It's only that I'm a little disappointed." I grinned flirtatiously at the concern he showed on his face.

"Disappointed, lass?"

"Yes, disappointed, I was hoping that as my gift you were going to finish that kiss you started yesterday."

He laughed, ripping the box from my hands as he tossed it onto the bed across the room and pulled me tightly against him. "Aye, I'll finish it, lass, and then I'll begin another and another."

This kiss held nothing of the shyness that had shown in his kiss the night before. His lips moved confidently against my own as one hand at the lower half of my back pulled me flush against him, his other hand winding its way into my hair.

I moaned as he pulled my lower lip deep into his mouth. He pulled away to speak breathlessly into my ear, the tickle of it causing me to squirm against him.

"Ach, lass. Doona make such a sound unless ye want me to take ye in that bed right there." He nudged his head in that direction.

While my body wanted nothing more than for him to do just that, something with Hew felt different. The feeling within me while in his presence was special, life-changing. It seemed that such a hasty act would cheapen my feelings for him. I laughed, his breath tickling my neck and back. "I'm sorry but I can hardly help it when you kiss me so."

"Do ye wish me to stop, lass?"

"No, not at all. I like your kisses very much." I kissed him, lightly allowing my tongue to slip inside before pulling away and was rewarded with him crushing me against him once more.

He devoured me, causing my head to grow light as we breathed each other's breaths as our own. If I didn't pull away and change the subject quickly, I would allow him to take me, and something in my mind screamed that this man needed to be different.

Slowly, I closed my mouth, giving him a small kiss before pulling away. "I just thought of something."

His green eyes were hazy, nearly blurred with the lust that I was certain mirrored my own eyes. "Aye? What is that, lass? Do ye think perhaps, ye could tell me later?"

I laughed and tried to step away, but he held me close to him. "No, it's very important. We have yet to name our puppies. We found them together. I think we should name them together."

He remained quiet for a moment. I suspected he was giving himself a minute to pull himself out of the thralls of his lustful thoughts. Slowly, he lessened the grip on my back and stepped away just slightly. "Aye, lass, ye are quite right. We should. I know what I wish to name the dark one."

"Really? What?"

"He's quite a masculine pup, do ye agree? His fur makes him look like an exotic beast. I think we should name him Tearlach. It means that he is a manly creature."

I smiled. I didn't think the puppy looked manly, only adorable, but he was right. As the pup grew, the fluffy hair around his head would make him look like a lion. "It's perfect."

"Ye should be the one to name the lighter one. 'Tis ye that found him."

I thought for a moment, but every name I thought of sounded too American. He needed a Scottish name that would fit his brother's. "Do you see how his tail always sticks up? It looks like he is waving a flag. Is there another word for that?"

"Aye, lass, I see. What about Bratach? It holds much the same meaning."

I stood on my tip-toes and kissed his cheek. "I think it's perfect, and with that I will take my leave. You are too much of a temptation for me to stay a moment longer."

He laughed his deep, grumbly laugh that shook his whole chest and made my knees go weak.

"Temptation, lass? Nay, 'tis ye that are the temptation. I have been alone for a long time. Ye have awakened feelings within me I fear I am too old to handle."

"You are not old. You're the same as me I'd imagine, and I am in no way old, which means neither are you." I moved to stand by the door.

"If you say so, lass. Will ye accompany me somewhere tomorrow afternoon?"

"Yes, I think I could manage that. Where?"

"'Tis a surprise, lass. I shall meet ye at the back of the castle come midday."

He opened the door to the cottage, taking my hand so that he could walk me back to the castle, leaving me to wonder just what tomorrow held in store for me.

Chapter 15

Hew rose early the next morning so that he could work on carving the large piece of wood remaining from the ornaments he'd made. He hoped to make it into a sort of sled that he and Adelle could take out on their outing this afternoon.

Just thinking about spending more time with her made his heart beat quickly. He'd lived alone for so long he'd convinced himself that it was the only way to honor the memory of his late wife, to stay trapped in the memories of his short time with her. But with each day since he'd met Adele, he felt more alive. He was slowly learning that nothing could have been further from the truth.

Mae had not been a jealous woman. She knew she held his heart and lived her life with more light and love than any other lass he'd ever met. She would've wished more for him. She wouldn't have been pleased that he'd spent so many years all alone.

It saddened him that for so long he'd not seen the truth in the mistakes he was making.

All he could do now was to try and move forward, living the rest of his life as Mae would've wished it. She would be very pleased to know that he'd found happiness once again. He could almost hear her whispering in his ear, pleading with him not to let her slip out of his grasp.

He didn't intend to let Adelle do any such thing, but he also knew it best that their afternoon spent together be passed out of doors. He was a man who'd gone too long without sharing his bed with another woman, and the next time he and Adelle were alone within four walls, he knew he would not be able to keep himself from claiming her as his own.

For this reason he worked, chipping away at the wood with as much force as he could muster, crafting it into the perfect seat for two. He was a man in need, and he needed to exert whatever physical activity he could to help keep his mind off her.

* * *

Either Hew hadn't told Mary what he planned for us to do this afternoon, or she was damned determined not to tell us what she knew.

Bri and Blaire had insisted on dressing me, and they'd decided to place me in the finest dress I had. "Are you sure this is appropriate? I feel very overdressed."

"It's always better to be overdressed than underdressed. I believe you are the one that taught me that. Besides, we have no way of knowing do we, since Mary refuses to tell us what his plans are?"

Bri continued to pick away at my hair, doing her best to pin it into place.

Mary threw her hands up in exasperation as she screamed angrily at us. "I already told ye, I doona know what his plans are. I havena spoken to him about it. Ye are a couple of thick-headed lassies, the two of ye!"

She turned and left us, stomping her feet on the way. Once she was gone, we both burst out into laughter. "I should not have pestered her so. There. What do you think?"

Bri stepped away so that I could turn and look in the mirror. "Thank you. My hair looks nice, but I feel ridiculous in this dress. I'd rather be in jeans and a nice blouse."

Bri laughed and bent down to squeeze me while placing her face up against my own. "I'm sure you would, but those days are over, I'm afraid. At least it's not expected that we shave our legs in this time."

"Thank God for small mercies." She was right. It would have been considered quite strange for us to do so in this time and that was fine with me. I always thought it a pain in the rear anyway.

"Are you nervous, Mom? You like him quite a lot, don't you?"

I stood, wishing I could shorten the dress a good eighteen inches just so I would be able to move more freely. "A little, but every time I'm around him whatever nerves I may have had before dissipate quickly. And yes, I like him very much, which is probably foolish. Once the snow melts, he'll no longer want to stay here."

"I wouldn't be so sure, Mom. I think if he had reason to stay, he would. You may just end up being that reason."

I hoped she was right. The thought of him leaving filled me with sadness, but I would not worry about that now. Today, I was simply going to enjoy his company.

Chapter 16

Damn Mary straight to hell; she'd known exactly what activity Hew had planned for us. When Hew arrived at the back entrance of the castle carrying a sled, I caught sight of Mary hiding around a corner, cackling like a banshee.

"It is not the least bit funny, Mary! Now, he will be forced to wait on me while I change. There's no way I'm going to get this dress sopping wet."

Mary stepped out from her place in the shadows, laughing as she waved her brother inside. "Oh, doona be such a grumpy bairn, Adelle. Hew, get yerself inside whilst the lassie changes."

Hew stomped his snow-covered feet off outside before following Mary's instruction, casting me an apologetic glance before reprimanding his sister. "'Twas no kind of ye, Mary." He turned to address me. "But I willna say I'm no pleased to see ye in such a fine dress, lass. Ye look lovely."

Mary piped up once again, not giving me a chance to thank him for his kind words.

"Ach, if ye find her pleasing in that, I'm sure ye shall fall over when ye see what she will come down in next. I'm certain she will use yer idea of playing in the snow as the perfect excuse to don her horrific garb from her own time. I doona see what the lads seem to see in it, but every time Adelle, Bri, or Blaire decide to squeeze themselves into their modern clothes, all the lads, me own Kip included, can hardly keep their tongues inside their mouths. 'Tis truly pathetic."

Hew's brows pulled together quizzically, but he said nothing. I ignored her as well and turned to make my way back upstairs.

I was almost out of sight when Mary called out to me. "I'm right, aye? Ye are going in search of yer 'jeans?'"

I smiled at the anticipation of ripping this burdensome dress of and sliding into the comfy denim. I screamed over my shoulder back at her. "Yes, Mary. You are very right, indeed."

* * *

Mary had also been right about Hew's reaction to seeing a woman in such clothing. It was certainly something men in this time were unaccustomed to. His mouth nearly fell open at the sight of me. Though entirely covered from head to toe, bundled up as much as I could for our snowy activities, I suddenly felt self-conscious under his gaze.

"Ach, lass, I doona know if ye should trust yerself with me when ye look as ye do. Do women truly dress in such a manner commonly where ye come from?"

I laughed and marched out into the snow ahead of him. "Oh yes, all of the time. This is quite a conservative outfit, I assure you. Would you rather I went and put my dress back on?"

He caught up to me quickly, throwing his arms around me from behind. He kissed me roughly on the cheek, his facial hair tickling my ear. "Nay, lass. I wouldna let ye go and change even if ye wished it. Come. I found a bonny hill near the cottage that shall be perfect for sledding."

Excited by his choice of activity, it rather surprised me as well. He was much more fun than he'd originally let on. Taking his hand in my own, we made our way to the snowy hill.

* * *

The lass meant to torture him. No other explanation for dressing the way she had made sense. He could make out the shape of her bum in her trousers, and what a fine bum it was. Round and full, just like a woman's should be.

If the lass spoke true, and there seemed no reason why she would not, he imagined men in her time spent a good portion of their days walking about quite uncomfortably, such a feast for their eyes laid out in front of them daily.

Hew breathed in deeply through his nose, hoping the chill in the air would cool the fire that burned inside him. Thankful when they reached the hill, he promptly placed the sled he'd built down into the snow and instructed Adelle to sit in the front so that he could join her on the back end.

Pushing off hard, they flew down the snowy landscape, both of them howling with delight as the cold wind rushed across their faces. When the sled finally reached the bottom of the hill, it stopped rather abruptly, uprooting both of them from their seats, sending them tumbling out into the snow.

They landed in a twisted pile. Adelle was on top of him laughing so hard that the trembling of her chest shook his own.

"Are ye all right, lass?" Their fun would be spoiled quickly if his idea caused her harm.

She smiled brightly, bending to quickly kiss him on the tip of his nose. He found himself wondering how a lass could manage to keep her teeth so brilliantly white. They were stunning, just like every other part of her.

"Yes, I'm fine. Let's go again!"

She leapt off of him and was halfway up the hill before he could manage to roll over and climb his way out of the snow.

Chapter 17

"Wakey, wakey..."

Bri's voice lured me out of a deep sleep. I awoke to find Bri and Blaire sitting on either side of me, grinning in anticipation.

I rolled onto my stomach, shielding my face from the both of them, groaning as I spoke. "What do you want? Just leave me alone. I'll wake up sometime tomorrow."

Bri stuck her hand into my hair, mussing it about so that I would turn back over onto my back. "You missed breakfast, so did Hew. Mary's not pleased with either one of you, and she said that you will just have to wait until evening to eat because she wasn't going to warm anything for you once you woke up."

I obliged her and rolled over, sitting myself up so that I was eye level with both of them. Endlessly hungry, I could out eat almost any man. No way would I wait until evening to eat. "Like hell I will. I am more than capable of feeding myself. That bossy biddy will not dictate when and what I eat."

Bri looked over at Blaire who laughed knowingly. "What did I tell you, Blaire? I knew she would say something like that."

I cleared my throat to draw her attention back to me. "Hicumm…excuse me. I'm right here you know. Now, what are the two of you doing in here?"

I knew well enough why they'd come, but Blaire obliged me by answering my question. "Why do ye think we have come? We wish to hear all about yer afternoon yesterday."

I couldn't help but grin thinking back on the day. It had been a wonderful afternoon and ages since I'd laughed so hard. My stomach would be sore for a week from the effort of it. I ached from head to toe, bruised from the many spills I'd taken into the snow, but every tight muscle was worth it. "Well, we honestly didn't do much of anything except sled down the giant hill near the cottage about a thousand times."

Bri smiled as she held onto her swollen belly. "Did you have a good time?"

"Aye, o'course she did. She canna keep from grinning." Blaire winked at me but pointed to my face in concern. "Ye seem to have had a wee bit too much fun though, Adelle. Ye are mighty red."

I reached up and touched my face, flinching at the pain. My cheeks felt quite swollen. There was little in the way of sunscreen in this time, and I'd not thought to cover my face, even after I learned we were to spend the day sledding. "Oh my, I'll have to see if Mary has any herbal salve I can put on this to calm it down a bit. How bad do I look?"

"Completely terrible."

My eyes widened in surprise. With each passing day Bri grew more uncomfortable in her pregnancy, and she was becoming increasingly blunt with her words. "Ouch. Thanks, Bri, but I suppose it's my own fault. I really didn't think about sunscreen at all."

Blaire glanced at Bri with shocked eyes and did her best to comfort me. "It isna all that bad, Adelle. It shall heal itself eventually."

"Eventually?" That was not okay with me. It needed to be completely healed by tonight. After our afternoon of sledding had concluded, Hew had very seriously and nervously asked that I dine with him in the cottage this evening. He said he had something very important he wished to tell me.

"Aye." Blaire looked at me nervously.

I knew it wasn't her fault, but she could tell I was agitated by her response that it would take some time to heal.

"I know that 'tis no pleasant for ye, but it shall take at least a week for ye to look like yerself I'm afraid."

"Awesome." I didn't know what else to say. Nothing could be done for my stupidity. I would look scary as hell when I arrived at the cottage this evening. Perhaps we could dine outside in darkness. Even if we both froze to death, it would be preferable to frightening the poor man to death with the abomination which was now my face.

* * *

"Are ye certain, brother? Ye havena known her verra long. 'Tis no small decision to decide to leave the home that ye have known for so long."

83

Hew moved about the cottage nervously. He knew it was a rash decision, but nothing had felt so right to him in a good many years. He loved the lass greatly, and he would tell her so tonight. "Aye, Mary, I am certain. There is naught left for me at home, and there hasna been since the day Mae left me. 'Twas foolish of me to stay there so many years after her death. It pains me to think on all the joy I have missed because I was too frightened no to be alone. I wasted much time."

His sister reached out and lay a comforting hand on his arm. "Nay, brother, ye dinna waste time. Things happen as they are meant to. If ye truly feel the way ye seem to about Adelle, then I doona believe ye were meant to leave yer home until now. If ye had, it wouldna have been her that ye found."

Mary's words comforted him. It was a kind way of thinking of all the mistakes he had made. Regardless, he was thankful that he had met the lass now. "Aye, Mary. I canna imagine no knowing the lass now. If I agree to work here at the castle, do ye think that Eoin and Arran shall agree to let me make this cottage me home?"

He smiled as Mary laughed. He should've expected such an answer from his fiery sister. "There is no need for ye to ask either of them. Ye are welcome to stay here because I say so and that's all the permission ye need. Both of the laddies know it and have since they were wee bairns. 'Tis I that am truly laird over Conall Castle."

"I believe ye are right, Mary. They all seem to bow at yer feet, regardless of the hard time ye seem to love to give them. Now, allow me to walk ye back to the castle, Lady Laird. I have much to think on. It will take me some time to think of just the right way to say what I must."

Chapter 18

"What in the bloody hell is the matter with ye, Adelle? Take that covering off the top of yer head."

I knew I looked ridiculous, like a cheap Halloween costume with the gauzy fabric over my head, but there was no way I was taking it off. I was a vain woman, and I wasn't afraid to admit it. Whatever he had to say to me, he could say it to me as I was or not at all. "No, I will do no such thing."

I stepped into the cottage past him, setting the growing Bratach on the floor as he went and joined Tearlach in their usual game of 'whose the toughest brother?'

He shut the door to the cottage and walked around to face me, frustration clear on his face. "Ye look ridiculous, lass. I wish to tell ye something important, and I doona wish to address ye covered like a wee ghost."

I glanced up at him, only barely making him out through the small holes in the fabric, but it allowed me to see his perfectly perfect face. I spoke a little more loudly than necessary. "How is your face not red as a beet? You were out in the same snow and under the same sun that I was in yesterday, and there is no sign of it anywhere on you!"

He laughed, understanding. "Ach, I see. Did the sun blister yer skin a bit, lass? I should have insisted that ye cover it, but I dinna think of it. I spend much of me days outdoors. I suppose it has grown accustomed to such sunlight."

"Well how wonderful for you. Let's eat." It wasn't only the way my face looked that put me in a sour mood, but the pain from it felt something awful. I'd never been burned so badly in my entire life.

"It shall be mighty hard for ye to eat properly with that covering ye. Just take it off, Adelle. Do ye really think that I'm so concerned with the way yer face looks?"

I nodded emphatically. "Of course you are. All men are."

He rolled his eyes, sat down at the table, and started eating immediately, not waiting for me to join him. He responded in between mouthfuls. "Suit yerself. Eat if ye wish. If ye truly believe that, Adelle, ye havena been around the right kind of men. I like yer face verra well, but 'tis no me favorite part of ye."

"Oh, fine. So you're a boob guy, I suppose? Maybe you prefer the 'arse?'" I mimicked his brogue, not sure why I felt the need to provoke him so.

"Yer 'boobs,'" the word sounded strange on his tongue, "and yer 'arse' are no so impressive, lass. 'Tis yer mouth that I enjoy verra much."

My brows met in the middle of my eyes underneath the veil. "My mouth? My lips are quite thin. You have strange tastes."

He stood and I thought perhaps I had pushed him too far.

"Aye? And ye are a bloody fool, Adelle. I dinna mean yer lips. I mean the shocking words that ye always seem to form with them. I have never known a lass so forward."

I looked down, embarrassed. "Yes. I know. That's always been a problem. It's a bit of a turn off, isn't it?"

He frowned once more and came to crouch down next to me, taking my hands into his. "I doona know what ye mean by 'turn off' but nay, I love the way ye speak verra much. Now, I willna tell ye what I must with that damned cloth covering yer head."

He yanked it away before I could grasp it. He reeled back in disgust, almost falling backward onto his bottom. "Ach, lass, ye look dreadful. Never ye mind, I doona wish to say what I once wished."

My eyes widened with shock and pain. He quickly scrambled up on his feet to gather me into his arms, laughing softly. "Oh, lass, forgive me. Doona look so upset. I couldna resist it after ye berated me such just a moment ago. Ye look mighty fine, lass. Ye always do."

I didn't pull away from him but rolled my eyes. "No, I do not honestly think I look fine. My face is so red I look like I was born on the sun, and it's quite swollen as well."

"Doona tell me what I think, lass. I wouldna lie to ye. I doona care if the redness never fades, although it shall. I would still think that ye looked mighty fine. Now, hush, and let me tell ye what I wished to when I asked ye to come here."

I relented. I didn't believe a word he said about my face at the moment, but I didn't wish to argue with him anymore. I was eager to hear what he had to say. "All right, fine. What is it?"

He stepped away and sat on the edge of the bed, holding my hands so that I would sit next to him. "I've decided that once the snow melts, I am no going to return home."

Hope fluttered in my chest. I'd spent every second trying not to think of the day when he would leave here and praying each night that the snow would stay forever. "Really? Why?"

"Do ye really no know the answer to that question, lass?"

He looked into my eyes. I could see all that he wished to say deep within them, but I desperately wanted him to say the words. "Maybe, but I won't know for sure until you tell me."

He took a deep, shaky breath. He was nervous, but I was not about to intervene and let him get away without saying what he felt. I'd let too many men do that before. If he meant it, he could find the strength to say the words. "I...I know that I havena known ye long, Adelle, but it doesna take so long for the heart to know what it wants. I'm in love with ye, lass. Verra much so."

I smiled, staring deep into his eyes, as tears I held back threatened to fall. I must have remained quiet for one moment too long for he spoke again, his voice shaky.

"I doona expect that ye should feel the same so quickly. Perhaps 'twas rash for me to tell ye so soon, but I have spent too many years alone. I willna deny meself love a moment longer if I can have it."

"No." I reached up and lay my hand against his cheek. "No. It wasn't too quickly at all. I love you too, Hew."

"Do ye truly, lass?"

"Yes, I do. I think I loved you the first moment I saw you in the snow, holding that sweet little puppy firm against your chest." I leaned forward and kissed him but had to pull away at the pain that shot through my lips at the pressure.

"Ach, lass. I'm verra sorry that ye are in such pain. Doona kiss me now. I hope there shall be plenty of time for that later."

"There's nothing for you to be sorry about, and yes I do too."

His face grew serious once more. For a moment I was worried.

"I willna return from where I came from, but before I make this me home, I must finish the journey I started. I must bid Mae farewell one last time, lass. I hope that ye doona mind."

I shook my head, surprised that he thought I might. "Of course I don't and of course you must. When will you leave?"

He looked out at the snow, black in the darkness, as he hesitated before answering. "At sunrise. I know that the snow isna melted yet, but it hasna snowed more in days. I am anxious to finish me journey so that I can begin a new chapter in me life."

Something twisted uncomfortably in my stomach, but I could not determine its source and did my best to push it from my mind. "You will be careful, yes?"

He smiled rubbing his hand gently up and down my back. "Aye, lass. Of course I will. I have something most precious that I must return to now."

*   *   *

I wished to stay with him until morning, but I left him shortly after learning he would leave at sunrise. I wanted him to be rested before travelling out in the snow. He'd sent both pups with me, leaving Tearlach in my care for the duration of his journey.

I slept fitfully. While I tossed wildly throughout the night, both pups slept soundly, snuggled tightly into my side in the bed with me. They didn't move all night, only rising right at sunrise. Just as the sun broke over the horizon, they stood on all fours in the bed. Looking toward the window in the direction of the cottage, they whined mournfully.

The knot in my stomach returned.

Chapter 19

Hew left right at sunrise just as he'd planned. It was not a far journey to Mae's resting place. In fair weather he could have made the trip there and back in a day, but with the snow still so deep, he knew it would take him at least two.

Just two days away from Adelle seemed too many. He wondered if she'd been disappointed that he hadn't asked her to marry him. He hoped she was not, for he intended to do so as soon as he made it back from bidding Mae one final farewell.

He wished to marry Adelle with all his heart, but some small piece of him would not allow himself to ask it of her when Mae still lingered in the back of his mind. He knew she would have been pleased for him. He'd come to that realization soon after he arrived at Conall Castle, but he wished to spend a few moments alone with Mae so that he could truly put the past behind him.

The day trickled by slowly as he lost himself in a sea of past memories. Memories of loneliness and the choices he'd made that had caused him to be so. A new future lay ahead of him. He couldn't wait to embrace it with all that he had.

He stopped often to allow his aging horse to rest and to clean the icy chunks from the horse's hooves and coat. He asked much of his beloved beast to accompany him on this trip. His horse was old. Hew knew the animal would not make it another year. It seemed appropriate that Greggory's last journey be the last time he would journey to Mae's grave, as well.

Slowly, dark descended over Hew and the great beast. He knew he should stop for the night, but no good place offered shelter from the snow. He knew there to be a small village just outside of the Conalls' territory. So against his better judgment, he nudged the horse on, praying with each soft kick of his heels that his companion could make it into the village.

It happened quickly. The horse stepped upon a rock buried out of sight, deep within the snow. He heard the creature's leg snap and did his best to throw his own leg over the side so that he could dismount before the animal fell, but Hew was not quick enough.

Just as he threw his leg over the side, Greggory fell in the direction he dismounted, pinning him beneath. As his own elbows sunk into the wet snow, they crashed roughly into the same rocks that had felled his horse. His left shoulder dislocated on impact.

Pain coursed through him. The weight of his horse on top of him knocked all the breath from his lungs. The stars in the sky melted together, turning into darkness as he lost consciousness.

* * *

Present Day

"Morna...Morna, wake up, lass!" Jerry shook his wife's shoulder with as much force as his thin arms could afford. He watched terrified as she tossed in her sleep, making noises as if she were injured. He could see her eyes darting back and forth beneath her closed eyelids, and he held his breath in fear until she opened her eyes to look at him.

"I must gather me spells. They are in need of us once more."

Jerry sighed in relief, his whole body trembling from the remnants of his worry. He'd seen his wife often stir during fits of her dreams, but never so much as he'd just witnessed. For a brief moment, he'd worried that it hadn't been magic that caused her to do so but perhaps old age.

He had every intention of passing from this life before his beloved. He knew he would not be able to live a day without her. "Ye scared me to death, Morna. I was afraid...well, I doona wish to speak of what I thought."

He smiled against her hand as she lay her palm against his cheek, knowing what he meant well enough. "'Tis not a worry ye should have. I shall no leave this world until I am good and ready to, and that willna be for a long time. Come."

She stood and waved at him to follow her. He did so without question. His wife carried a great burden, one he was eternally grateful he didn't possess. "What is it, lass?"

"A lad I knew as a child has taken a fancy to Adelle, and he finds himself in need of help. I must warn them, send Adelle the dreams that were just shown to me so they may have a chance of reaching him in time."

She didn't stop to explain more to him, and he didn't ask any further questions. This was an urgent matter, but he didn't worry over such things as his wife did. He'd yet to see one of her spells go awry.

Chapter 20

I'd slept so little the night before Hew departed that I would have been on edge the next day even if the pups had not chosen the exact moment of his departure to whine as if wounded. I spent the entire next day sick with worry, and it exhausted me. My only relief was that my face no longer ached, and the swelling had diminished greatly throughout the day.

As I travelled upstairs to my bedchamber, a pup under each arm, I was sure I would spend another sleepless night worried over Hew. Much to my surprise, a sense of drowsiness so strong that I felt halfway asleep by the time I reached my bedchamber door overcame me.

It seemed a great effort to change into my nightgown. As soon as my head hit the pillow, I fell asleep.

* * *

I woke in the middle of the night with sweat beaded on my brow. The covers were off of the bed, mangled on the floor as if I had fought a great battle in my sleep. Screaming had pulled me out of the horrific dream I was having, and for a moment I thought I had heard my own yells.

I felt the need to scream now. Visions of Hew crushed beneath the weight of his horse, unable to scoot from beneath the animal, burned in my mind. I stilled in the bed, sitting up so that I could listen.

For a moment all remained quiet, but it took only a second before another scream ripped through the castle corridors.

I leapt out of the bed. Bri. She must have gone into labor sometime in the night. I could only hope that it was just starting, and I had not missed being there for her.

I burst into her and Eoin's bedchamber, relieved to see that Mary was already making preparations, ordering others about while Blaire administered Morna's mixture to Bri.

I ran to her side, giving her my hand as she squeezed it tightly with an incoming contraction. "How are you? Is everything well?"

She grunted in between words, determination set in her face. She was beyond ready to get the child out of her. "Yes, as well as it can be, I believe. Will you get out there and tell Eoin he better get his ass in here this second? I don't give a damn it it's unusual for men to stay at the bedside during delivery. If he misses the birth of his child, I shall never forgive him."

"Of course." I had to pry her fingers loose and turned to Mary only briefly before leaving. "Is she close, or do we have some time before the baby arrives?"

Mary must have been able to tell something else distressed me for she answered me quickly, waving me on to whatever other task sat on my mind. "Nay, she isna as close as she wishes. We have some time still."

I nodded and ran out of the bedchamber, nearly running into the three men – Eoin, Arran, and Kip – huddled together in the hallway. I knew I must do as Bri bid first. Although I was certain my dream had meant something, I couldn't know for sure that what I had seen had been real.

I grabbed Eoin's arm and pulled him away from the circle, smacking him lightly as I scolded him. "What on earth do you think you are doing? You better get in there with Bri right this instant or I am going to drag you there myself."

He looked back at me nervously. "I am afraid to, Adelle. I doona think I can bear to see her in such pain, and I couldna live with the guilt if something happened to her and the babe."

I softened, feeling sorry for him. It was easy for women to forget what a terrifying ordeal childbirth was for the father. "Nothing is going to happen to them. Morna's drink will help with the pain soon and all will go well. Trust me, if you miss this, Bri will not understand. Go. Now."

He nodded and hurried down the hall, leaving me to turn my attention to Arran and Kip. "I need to ask something of both of you. I know that you may think me mad, but please I beg you, listen to me before you dismiss me."

Kip stood silently, giving me an expression that I knew meant he dreaded whatever I was about to tell him. He knew it would only mean more work for himself.

Arran nodded and reached out to lay a reassuring hand on my shoulder. "Aye, of course, Adelle. What is it?"

"I had a dream, a terrible one. I've never had one quite so vivid. It was dark, and Hew was lying on his back in the snow. His horse had fallen on top of him, crushing him, and one of his arms hung oddly to his side." Saying what I'd seen out loud made it seem more real to me. As I finished, my voice cracked. I couldn't keep a tear from falling down my face.

Arran glanced quickly at Kip and then back at me. "Do ye think that he is in danger, lass, or did ye only have a dream that has upset ye?"

I shook my head. "I don't know, but I'm afraid that he might be. I know it seems crazy."

Arran squeezed the shoulder he held under his hand. "Nay, it isna crazy. We have all seen too much of what Morna can do to think so. Kip and I will ride at once."

"Thank you. I'm sorry to send you, but I can't leave Bri right now."

Arran was already moving down the corridor, Kip following silently behind him as he called back to me. "Of course you canna. Doona worry. We shall find him in time."

I believed that they would. They had to. I couldn't bear to think otherwise.

Chapter 21

Once Morna's medicine worked its way through Bri's system, her screams lessened substantially and things began moving rather fast.

She dilated more quickly than Mary had expected. Much to her dismay, she was forced to enlist the help of each of us to help in some way. Blaire did whatever Mary asked of her while Eoin and I set on either side of Bri, coaching and calming her with each set of pains.

When it came time for Bri to push, I watched in awe and astonishment at her strength. It was a miraculous thing. The love that filled the room in the moment the tiny bundle arrived into this world was enough for me to momentarily push away my worries over Hew.

While here, there was nothing I could do, and my heart nearly burst through my chest when I held my granddaughter in my arms for the first time.

I'd heard it said before that grandchildren filled you with a kind of love that was not even matched by your children. I'd always thought it a crazy notion, but as I latched on to her tiny fingers, I finally understood.

To hold a little human, one that came from a very piece of me, allowed me for an instant to believe that I would truly live on forever, in Bri, in her daughter, and in whatever children this child would one day have. It was all that one could ask for in life, more than I ever thought I would receive.

"Mom, you're crying more than I am, more than Eoin."

I glanced over to see Eoin practically blubbering in the corner and laughed as I carried the child to Bri's loving arms. "I don't care. I have never seen anything more perfect in my entire life."

Bri smiled, bending to kiss her daughter's head. "I know. Me either. Where's Arran? I'm sure he's ready to meet his niece."

I didn't wish to burden any of them with bad news, but I knew I must tell them. "It's nothing to worry over I'm sure, but I had a dream about Hew. I became worried that perhaps something had happened to him on his journey. Arran and Kip rode after him to make sure that he is all right."

Bri looked up at me, clearly seeing past the calm façade I was doing my best to put on. "Go."

I shook my head, dismissing her. "No, I'm not going to leave you so soon. You just had a baby for goodness sakes."

She raised her left hand and shooed me from the room. "Mom, go. Everything is fine here. I know you need to be there. Just promise me you'll be careful."

I couldn't deny she was right. I bent quickly to kiss her and the babe on the forehead before turning to leave the room. "I will."

I ran to the stables, mounting the first horse I saw and took off at full speed away from Conall Castle.

101

Chapter 22

I'd left the castle before sunrise, and it neared dusk when I found them. The vision before me was just as I'd seen it in the dream. I had been right. I was certain it was Morna who'd sent it to me.

"Is he…" I could hardly force the words out of my mouth. "Is he alive?"

"Aye, lass. I am verra alive and intend to stay that way."

When Hew's voice answered, the relief that washed through me was enough to nearly bring me to my knees.

My legs were shaky as I approached him, the adrenaline that had allowed me to ride to him so quickly suddenly receding. I knelt next to him, grabbing both sides of his face as I examined him for injuries. I spoke to Arran and Kip behind me, "Why haven't you moved the horse off of him? He's going to lose his legs if the horse stays on him much longer."

"We only just arrived as well, lass. Ye must have been riding verra quickly to have caught us."

Hew reached his right hand up to touch my face. The other arm still dislocated. "Nay, lass. If I hadna thrown me shoulder out of place, I would have been able to scoot out from under him. I willna lose me legs."

"I'm glad to hear it." I stepped out of the way so that Arran and Kip could get on either side of him. Together they lifted him, avoiding his injured shoulder so that they could pull him out from under the horse whose breathing was shallow. My heart winced in sadness at the creature's pain. His suffering would have to be ended.

Once his legs were free, Arran had me move to Hew's right side so that I could hold him down and steady while Kip secured his feet. Once he was as still as we could get him, Arran asked him to bite a rag as he jerked the shoulder into place. It was a horrible sound but after the initial pain, the relief became instantly visible on Hew's face.

With help, the two men pulled him to his feet. After a few moments of allowing his blood to re-circulate, he moved about to get his footing under him.

Eventually, he turned to address all of us. "I am verra grateful for yer help. I hate to ask it of ye, but would ye all mind riding ahead a ways, only for a few moments?"

"Why?" The word slipped out quickly, but as I looked at the way he stared down at his horse, sadness in his eyes, I knew.

"It must be I that end this for him, and I wish to do it alone."

Silently, we turned and left him.

He'd not taken long. Once he joined us, we made plans to stay in the village where Hew was heading when his horse had fallen. Close to Mae's grave, Hew was determined to complete the journey he had intended.

Although I couldn't stand the thought of leaving him alone once again, I understood his need to do this one last time.

* * *

Arran, Kip, and I had been at the small inn a few hours when Hew arrived. He said little as he entered, only asking which was his room and leaving us in the dining hall to retire for the evening.

We followed him shortly, separating as we each made our way to our rented rooms. We were all exhausted. I couldn't blame him for not wishing to speak with us when he'd arrived. I was just happy to know that he was safe.

He'd suffered much the last few days. He was sure to be sore, tired, and heartsick at the loss of his beloved horse, not to mention the melancholy I knew he must feel after having visited Mae's grave.

For this reason I expected it to be Arran or Kip at the door when I heard a soft knock right as I had blown all but the last candle out for the evening. Instead, when I opened the door, Hew stood before me, his eyes hungry and in need.

Chapter 23

"You should be in bed. You're injured and it's been a long day."

He didn't answer me, only moved into the room shutting the door behind him. He reached out to me with his good arm, pulling me close to him as he kissed me desperately.

After a moment, he pulled away breathlessly. "Doona tell me what I should do, lass. I had to see ye."

He released me and I stepped away, hoping that putting some distance between us would dim the fire he'd lit within me. It did nothing to help. "Is everything all right?"

"Aye, lass. Will ye marry me?"

The words caught me off guard. He spoke them so quickly, I wondered for a moment if perhaps he hadn't meant to say them. "What? What did you just say?"

It took him only two strides until he stood before me, clasping tightly onto both of my hands. "Ye did hear me, lass, but I shall ask ye again. Will ye marry me, Adelle?"

A pleading in his eyes nearly broke my heart. After everything, he still worried that I might say no. "Yes, of course."

"Really, ye will, lass?"

"Aye," I mimicked his brogue in jest, reaching up to kiss him gently before standing on my tip-toes to whisper into his ear. "I want nothing more than to be your wife."

At once, the hunger I had seen in his eyes when I opened the door returned. He kissed me wildly with no sort of restraint. He held me flat against him as he groaned into my mouth and dug his hips into me. I moaned at the sensation.

"I'm verra pleased to hear it, for I dinna wish to bed ye if ye werena to be me wife. Now that ye are, I doona believe I can wait until we are married. But I willna touch ye if ye doona wish it."

"You're joking, right?" My fingers immediately flew to help him in the removal of his shirt. It felt like I'd been waiting years to see what lay beneath it, and I couldn't help the sharp intake of breath the sight of him caused me. He was beautiful, perfect, and now he was mine.

He laughed at my hastiness. "Tit for tat, lass. Turn yerself around."

He did his best to untie my laces, but his shoulder was still so sore that he could scarcely use one of his hands. "Go get in the bed," I demanded.

He shook his head, taking my order for a dismissal of his ability to make love due to his injuries. "Nay, lass. I am well enough to bed ye. Thinking of doing so was the only thing that kept me from succumbing to the icy cold that tried to lure me into death. I doona care if me shoulder bothers me. I need to be inside ye, Adelle."

106

"Oh, don't worry. You will be. Take off your clothes and go get in the bed."

He laughed but obeyed. I had to restrain from reaching out to smack his beautiful rear end as he took of his clothes. There was age to his body, no doubt, but I wouldn't have wanted him any other way. To me, it only added to his masculinity.

"Ye are a bossy wench, are ye no?"

I didn't answer him, only grinned wickedly and nodded, as I slowly untied my laces. I reveled in the way his jaw dropped with every increasing inch of skin that revealed itself to him as I slowly removed my dress.

I gave him a moment to gaze upon me, the adoration in his eyes enough to make me feel as if I was the most beautiful woman on earth. I moved across the room to blow out the last candle. As darkness engulfed the room, I slipped inside the bed with him, straddling myself atop him to care for his tender shoulder.

I leaned forward, my bare breasts pressing up against his chest. I kissed him, moaning as he dug his fingers deep into my hair and tugged my head backward, exposing my neck as he kissed me along my collarbone.

I squirmed astride him and when he could stand it no more I raised up so that I could descend upon him. We moved together gently, both of us absorbed in the newness of one another.

It didn't matter that the candles weren't lit, the room was ablaze with our love for one another.

Chapter 24

We were married in the great room of Conall Castle on New Year's Day surrounded by all of the people we loved most in the world. The vows were simple, but I'd never meant anything more than the few words we spoke to one another.

"I doona know where life will take me, but I choose ye to be at me side. From this day forward, me soul belongs to naught but ye. I now bind meself to ye in the present and for all the times to come. Together we are now one."

I didn't know where the vows came from and I'd undoubtedly messed up the accent badly, but Hew didn't care and neither did I.

As he leaned in to kiss me, baby Ellie Adelle Conall, named in honor of Eoin's mother, Elspeth and myself, squealed as if she'd been pinched. Our pups howled loudly in response.

A happy chaos surrounded us, and it was just as we wished it.

I had been right. It proved to be the best Christmas that Conall Castle had ever seen.

About the Author

Bethany Claire is the author of the Scottish, time-traveling romance novels *Morna's Legacy Series,* which includes the novels *Love Beyond Hope, Love Beyond Reason,* and her debut novel, *Love Beyond Time.* She lives in the Texas Panhandle.

Connect with me online:

http://www.bethanyclaire.com
http://twitter.com/BClaireAuthor
http://facebook.com/bethanyclaire
http://www.pinterest.com/bclaireauthor

If you enjoyed reading *A Conall Christmas,* I would appreciate it if you would help others enjoy this book, too.

Recommend it. Help other readers find this book by recommending it to friends, readers' groups and discussion boards.

Review it. Please tell other readers why you like this book by reviewing it at the retailer of your choice. If you do write a review, please send me an email to bclaire@bethanyclaire.com so I can thank you with a personal email, or you can visit my website at http://www.bethanyclaire.com

Join the Bethany Claire Newsletter!
Sign up for my newsletter to receive up-to-date information of books, new releases, events, and promotions.

http://bethanyclaire.com/contact.php - mailing-list

Acknowledgments

Every book, whether it be a full-length novel or a shorter novella such as this could never be completed without the help of many, many people.

Mom, you will always be the person to whom I owe the most thanks. Your endless encouragement, patience, and hours reading and re-reading are just a few of the reasons I love you more than anyone in this world. You're my best friend, and I think we make a phenomenal team.

Abbie, for the late-night chats and sodas. You have provided endless comic relief when I needed it most. Thanks for the stress-relief.

To the rest of my family: Dad, Maegan, Montana, Charlie & Flag, little stories of ours will work their way into every book I'm certain. Thanks for the inspiration.

To DeWanna, for the suggestions.

As always to my team members: xuni.com, Damonza.com, and Rik Hall formatting.

Other Books by Bethany Claire

Morna's Legacy Series

Love Beyond Time
Love Beyond Reason
A Conall Christmas – A Christmas Novella
Love Beyond Hope
Love Beyond Measure
In Due Time – A Novella (September 2014)

CPSIA information can be obtained at www.ICGtesting.com
Printed in the USA
BVOW08s0326211215

430707BV00005B/763/P